# Cricklewood Cowboys

## By

## Tom O'Brien

Published by Tomtom Theatre

## Authors Note

Cricklewood Cowboys is a work of fiction. Most of the events depicted did happen however, though not necessarily in the manner described. None of the characters exist- although this was the London of the author and many of his friends. The reader may wish to speculate which, if any, of the characters most resemble the author, and which, if any, of the events relate to him. Any similarity to other living persons is purely intentional.

# Chapter One

It wasn't such an earth-shattering experience as I thought it might be, the day I was banged up for eighteen months. The judge who sentenced me gave me a stern lecture on the abuse of trust and the sanctity of other peoples' property then said the public had a right to protection from people like me. I thought the ould fucker was going to give me five years, so the eighteen months came as a bit of relief. He also said I should be deported at the end of my sentence, which upset me more than the deprivation of my freedom. The bird I could do standing on my head, but…I had been slung out of a few places in my time, but never a country.

The two months I had spent on remand in Brixton had been easy-going, but Wandsworth was something else. Dark and foreboding, it was a Dickensian shambles of a place. 'Get those clothes off…get cleaned up…' the reception screw shouted as we filed past him, filtering us through a disinfecting process that was similar to sheep-dipping. Some of the dirtier inmates were poked and prodded with long-handled loofahs as they shuffled along the line.

Afterwards, I was paraded in front of the prison doctor, who felt my pecker before passing me fit for general duties. All my worldly possessions - one Timex watch and ten shillings and sixpence - were then sealed in a grubby brown envelope and my name and number written across it, and I was issued with my prison kit. A couple of John Players - which I had concealed in my hair - slipped to the reception con, ensured that the clothes fit me. It was only when the heavy steel door to my cell slammed shut that it hit home I wouldn't be seeing daylight for some time to come.

-

Prison mornings are not for the faint -hearted. Doors kicked and slammed open, steel landings echoing to the ring of hob-nailed boots, yells from every direction: 'Right you lot, slop out! The wing I was billeted on had four landings, each with its own recess for getting rid of the shit and piss accumulated during the night. The stench was unbearable. It lingered for hours - long after the cleaning crews had done their bit. I thanked God I was on the topmost landing; the contents of some of the pots never made it to the sinks, but were tipped over the railings into the void below.

No inmate was allowed to keep a razor blade in his cell. Each morning the landing screw issued a blade from the folder he carried with him. If you were lucky, it might be the one you used the previous day.

The cell housed a steel bunk bed along one wall and a single frame bed along the other. You weren't allowed to lie on the bunk bed during the day, and the single bed had to be dismantled and stood against the cell wall each morning. The bed linen had to be folded in a certain way, and if the screw didn't like your handiwork, he tipped it on to the floor and made you re-do it. There were three small lockers, three chairs and a single table.

Each prisoner was allocated one pot, one plastic jug, one mug, plastic cutlery, one razor, one pair of boots, one pair of slippers, two pairs of socks, two vests, two shirts, one jacket, one tie, one soap dish, one toothbrush, and a copy of the prison rules.

Outside each cell was fixed a small card rack containing information on its occupants. Name, prison number, work category, religion and length of sentence. It soon became apparent to me why the place was such a shit hole: It was inhabited mostly by dossers, tramps and petty thieves, all short -term occupants, who, when released, did their best to get back inside again.

I soon discovered that tobacco was the currency the prison ran on. All those little extras that made life bearable - that extra pair of socks, the jacket that fitted, yesterday's newspaper, a not-so-used copy of Playboy - they all had their price. Every Friday the money you earned could be spent in the prison shop, and items such as tobacco, soap and toothpaste could be purchased. You could buy up to a half ounce of tobacco, and this was the first item you purchased - whether you smoked or not. You could then sell it or trade it for something else, gamble with it or, if you were hard enough, become a tobacco baron. I usually bought soap or toothpaste with what was left over, the prison soap being vile and the toothpaste only fit for scouring your pisspot.

In due course, I was allocated work in the mailbag shop; a long, narrow workshop where the seating arrangements resembled those in a school. One screw prowled the centre aisle, whilst another sat on a platform overseeing everything. We weren't allowed to smoke during work, and the mobile screw's main function appeared to be to shout 'one off, Mr Beasley' to his seated companion each time one of us requested permission to go to the bog. We weren't supposed to smoke in there either, but they didn't seem too bothered about it. I thought it hilarious that they had to address each other as 'mister'.

My companion during working hours was Derek, and it was only natural that we should talk. Or to be more accurate, Derek did. Non-stop. About trucks. Big trucks. Enormous bloody trucks. Fucking boring trucks. He expected the rest of the world to have an orgasm when he talked about his Scannia. At first I

6

thought Scannia was his wife. After a while I perfected a nodding technique, which allowed me to concentrate on more important matters. Like how much time I had left to do: two months on remand…a third off for good behaviour…that still left another ten months. I couldn't take ten months of Derek and his jabber. Then I read on the notice-board of a welding course in a nick up the country, so I put my name down for it. A few weeks later I learnt that my application was successful.

-

HMP Mousehold was classed as semi-open. The main block didn't look much different than Wandsworth; a big, rambling, decaying construction, but there was another section known as The Huts. These were Nissan huts, each holding twenty in a dormitory environment. Each was self-sufficient, the occupants being responsible for cleaning and maintaining it. We fetched our grub from the main hall, and apart from roll-call each morning and evening, were left mainly to our own devices.

Our hut was reserved for those on the welding course. Strangeways, Barlinni, Camp Hill, they were all represented. Most were English; there was a sprinkling of Taffys and Jocks, and myself the only Irishman. There were no Blacks, which surprised me considering the numbers I had seen in Brixton and Wandsworth.

I was known as Paddy despite my repeated attempts to furnish my real name. In the end I gave up. The best response to a taunt of 'what's a thick Mick like you doing on a welding course?' was to shout back 'the same as you, you scabby Limey cunt'.

Jet Lag was one of the characters on the course. A recidivist of more than twenty years standing, his presence was the result of a prank. He had applied for a gardening course, but not being able to read and write too well, had asked somebody else to fill in the form for him. 'Jesus Paddy', he said to me one day, 'what do I want to learn welding for?' The authorities didn't care one way or the other; a welding course he had put down for, a welding course he would do.

Lefty, whose bunk was next to mine, was doing two years for hijacking a lorry-load of shoes. Unfortunately for him, the consignment consisted entirely of left shoes, something which caused much amusement amongst the rest of us. 'Is there a big one-legged population in Bethnal Green then, Lefty?' 'Found yourself a niche in the market, Lefty? ' 'The Old Bill reckoned you didn't have a leg to stand on'…

7

For my own part, I found myself up before the Governor within days of my arrival. My appeal against my deportation had been turned down. I had hoped that common sense might prevail; I mean, what was the point of teaching me a trade then chucking me out? But bureaucracy knows no logic.

'However', the Governor waffled on, 'it's no concern of this establishment that an expulsion order has been served on you. Our job is to see that you complete your sentence here. You will then be released in the normal manner. What happens after that is up to the appropriate authorities...'

Fuck me, I thought... would it be too much to hope that the matter might slip their minds altogether?

-

Life in the dormitories was a million miles from prison life in many ways. The dreaded slopping-out routine for one thing, the constant banging of doors, the turn of a key in the lock. In certain respects it was like being in the army - if you kept the rules the screws never bothered you much.

Yet when the lights went out at night, and you lay there looking out at the lit-up walls with their coils of razor wire on top, you were forced to admit that your dreams of freedom were just an illusion. I would watch the twinkling stars overhead, see the glare from the city of Norwich hanging like a shroud above the wire, and imagine the hordes of people out there. All drinking, fighting, making love, living life unfettered. And I felt a lump in my throat.

Then I pictured Tessa lying in Larry's arms, could almost smell the betrayal, and somehow it didn't seem too bad where I was. I killed them all in my fantasies. A thousand times over. Tessa I saved the worst fate for; she had made a fool of me and that was hard to forget. Sometimes I thought of Fergus, deep in the cold and lonely soil, his eyes open and reproachful.

I hardly thought of my parents at all; didn't know if they knew where I was, didn't really care. I received no letters, I wrote none. I retreated into a world of imagination. In reality, I was lying on my bunk staring at something on the ceiling, but in my mind I was lying on the beach in San Tropez, or trekking across the Arizona desert. Years later, when I read Papillon, I was able to understand how its author, Henri Charriere, managed to survive the French penal colonies. He wasn't really spending his years in a rat-infested dungeon that got flooded at every high tide; he was out walking the world of his imagination.

When I wasn't in foreign lands, I was learning to weld. I had no desire to pursue it as a trade - it was just something to pass the time - but our tutor had

8

other ideas. Day after day, week after week, he kept us at it, so that by the end of the course even Jet Lag could fuse two bits of metal together.

At the end of the course I was assigned to one of the tradesmen screws.

'Done a plumbing?', he asked me the first morning.

I shook my head. We had been assigned to the screw quarters outside the gate, and I was busy re-discovering that long-legged women in short skirts were real, not just images I had wanked myself silly over for the past ten months.

'Well, never mind. Once you've done one it will be a piece of cake...'

It was too. I discovered that all we were doing was renewing the taps on the sinks and baths in each flat, something that took very little time and effort. Not that we seemed to be in any great hurry.

'Don't get carried away, lad. This has to last us at least a month...'

There was no better man for making easy work look hard. Hadn't I years of practice...

The arrangement was that I would do upstairs and he downstairs, so I was left more or less to my own devices. I began to take books with me to put down the time. If I wasn't going to work myself to death, I might as well learn something. It was better than wanking myself to death I concluded, thinking of all the starched hankies under my pillow.

I was alternating between reading Borstal Boy and The Ginger Man when it suddenly clicked what had been niggling me. Barney Berry, one of the characters in Donleavy's book was none other than Behan himself!. I speculated on whether they had known each other; Behan rolling in and out of places such as McDaids or Mary The Whore's, Donleavy following along making notes...

Or maybe he was rolling too... Sebastian Dangerfield....now who was he based on?

You had to hand it to Behan. All his life he had been a drunkard, a layabout and a loudmouth - but he could write. And he had the gift of the gab.

Reporter: 'What do you think of Canada, Mr Behan?'

'Ah, 'twill be grand when it's finished'.

'And what do you think of the Irish?'

'Ah sure, God love them, if 'twas raining soup they'd be out with knifes and forks'.

Maybe I liked him because he was working class. A house painter that had seen the gutter, had lain in the gutter, and hadn't been afraid to write about it. His description of the Dublin slums was something I could relate to. I had seen poverty too, albeit in a rural environment. But when it came down to it, there wasn't much difference between stealing turnips from a market barrow or a farmer's field. His book about his time in Borstal was riveting

Between the bouts of working and reading there was plenty of fags and coffee to be had. I got the impression that some of the women liked having me around the house. It was just that little bit...risky. Maybe it turned them on; there were sometimes glimpses of thighs and stocking-tops, or a blouse undone a button more than was necessary. Let's face it, most of their husbands were miserable bastards, and they were stuck in this hole just as much as any of us prisoners - with little hope of remission.

I was trying to crack the seal on a stubborn pipe beneath the washbasin one morning when I noticed her standing there. The woman of the house, looking down at me. She had a cup of coffee in one had; the other was resting on her hip.

'Do you know how to use that King Dick?' she suddenly asked.

The monkey wrench fell from my grasp and I could only nod.

She knelt down beside me and placed a hand on my thigh.

'That's alright then. Only my husband hasn't got a clue about...things like that'.

She knew about King Dicks alright. Before I could say a word she had unzipped me and was squatting over me, her hands gripping the edge of the basin to give her leverage. It didn't take too long. The next morning - and most subsequent ones - I returned to the flat for what we now called my 'elevenses'. The screw, I learned, was also occupied. She told me he was conducting affairs with several of the women. I never found out who, though, because he never talked about it. It was as if our sessions with the women never took place; he showed me the flats we were to work on each morning - and that was it.

I sometimes thought of him as screw who did a bit of plumbing, but mostly it was as a plumber who did a bit of screwing. I could see now why he wanted to drag the job out. Afterwards, I wondered why the wives indulged in this little game of theirs. I didn't flatter myself that I was the only one singled out; there were other gangs - carpenters and painters - and I was sure they got similar privileges. It had to be because of boredom; it was a dreary fucking hole if you didn't have to be there; 'having it off' with a prisoner was their way of bringing a bit of excitement into a drab existence.

Christmas, normally one of the loneliest times in prison, didn't bother me at all. Most of my Christmas's since leaving home had been shitty anyway. Seeing all that happiness on the faces of others made me want to puke. There was a festive air about the prison; the screws even locked you up with a smile. It amused me to see slices of turkey, Brussels sprouts, roast potatoes and plum pudding all heaped together on one steel tray. But not so much as to make me want to ape Jet Lag, who alternated a forkful of meat and gravy with one of pudding. There was even some hooch, brewed from ingredients spirited out of the kitchen. A small glass of it immobilized Lefty and had him howling like a dog on the floor. After that we diluted it.

I even got religion for the day, attending Mass. Religion was optional here. Not like Wandsworth - where I tried to have atheist written on my cell card. 'You have to have a religion', the landing screw had insisted, so I put down Jehovah Witness. This meant I was effectively excused religious duties, there being no service for this particular sect. Instead, I took a perverse satisfaction at watching Songs of Praise on Sunday nights, following the camera as it panned over the unsuspecting audience. I would select the most angelic face I could find and invest it with the vilest characteristics I could dream up.

The highlight of Christmas day was the concert, put on by a bunch of local do-gooders. It was beyond me that people were willing to give up their boozing and celebrating to come and entertain us.

'They must be facking mad', said Lefty, who, like most of us, had put in an appearance only in the hope of seeing a bit of tit or leg on display.

Soon it was New Year and before I knew it I was on my last week. I hadn't really thought much about freedom before, but now that it was staring me in the face I became apprehensive. What would I do? Where would I go? I felt no different about life then when I came in, so what had it taught me? I was wiser perhaps, but I felt no better for the experience.

Was I a hardened criminal? I doubted it. Hardened criminals were a bit of a myth in Mousehold as far as I could see. The system weeded out the real hard cases and sent them to where they could act like James Cagney. Most of the cons I was acquainted with were like myself - lonely and mixed up. They missed their wives, their girlfriends, their families. Some got 'Dear- John' letters and cracked up. Sometimes they didn't get them and still cracked up. And sometimes the screws didn't wait for them to crack up, but banged them up in chokey before giving them the letter. Some were like Jet Lag; pathetic no-hopers who couldn't make up their minds where the real world lay - inside or outside. Me? I had no doubts. I wasn't planning to come back.

The afternoon before my release I said goodbye to all my friends. I was then taken to reception to return all my prison belongings. In return, I received my

Timex watch, ten shillings and sixpence, a travel warrant and my own clothes. To be fair to the prison, they had cleaned and pressed my dark suit and cream shirt, so that I was leaving cleaner than when I arrived. I felt nearly human again as I was taken to the holding area to await my freedom next morning.

At seven am the gates clanged shut behind the group of us that been freed. Loved ones, friends who had been holding a dawn vigil, surged forward to kiss and hug us. Two burly coppers greeted me. They didn't hug or kiss me, but re-arrested me and told me I was being escorted to Heathrow for deportation.

-

It had never occurred to me before, but I realised I was afraid of flying. I had never seen the inside of a plane before; all I knew was that passengers climbed steep steps, disappeared inside those enormous bellies, and that was it. For all I knew they could be eaten alive once inside.

Well It was too fucking late now, I was flying whether I liked it or not.

My two companions, seated either side of me in this greasy spoon, were there to ensure that I did. Deported, slung out on my ear, the ignominy of it. I had done my time, paid my debt to society, why couldn't they leave it at that? What had I ever done to England to deserve the big boot in the arse? And why couldn't it be by boat? It was good enough for Brendan Behan.

'D'you want a sandwich Paddy?' one of the coppers asked me. His heavy blue tweed overcoat contrasted sharply with my own lightweight suit. I could see the fields through the window, grey with frost. Jesus, my knackers were about to drop off.

'What county are we in?' I asked, washing down the greasy bacon with sweet tea.

'Bedfordshire', came the reply.

I looked around. Flat, barren land as far as the eye could see.

'It must be the arsehole of England then'. I laughed at their proximity to me. Any nearer and they'd both be sitting on my lap. 'Afraid I might make a run for it? Where would I hide? Under a stone?'

They both laughed then the older one took out a packet of Embassy and offered them round.

'Only doin' our job, Pat. We have to make sure you get on that plane. We don't want no slip-ups, see?'

I took several deep drags. There hadn't been many of them in the past year.

'What age are you, Paddy?' It was the younger ones turn now.

'Twenty-four'.

'Got any family?'

'I had a brother but he's dead'. Poor Fergus.

''I expect your mum and dad'll be glad to see you'.

I nodded, but inside I knew it wasn't true. I hadn't spoken to my old man for more than five years. And my mum, well…since Fergus died I had no idea how she might be feeling towards me.

'What devilish crime did you commit? It must be something big to get you chucked out…'

I shrugged. 'I robbed a few pubs is all' A few thousand quid I could do with right now.

He shook his head. Couldn't understand it, he said.

'Still, you must have it stashed away, eh?'

I laughed. 'I gave it all to William Hill'. I had too. Every fucking penny.

'Gambling? So that's what got you into this mess?'

I nodded. 'Fast women and slow horses'. It was mostly the latter though. The only fast woman around was Tessa…

The older one stubbed his butt on his saucer. 'Here's some free advice, lad. Keep your money in your pocket. Only one lot get rich from gambling - and it's not mugs like you. My uncle gambled everything he owned - and quite a lot that he didn't - and he wound up jumping off the Mersey Bridge….'

I had heard it all before. Same song... different singer. There was a long-playing record of it spinning permanently inside my head. Still, it passed the time till we got to Heathrow. Boarding time soon came round, where the sight of my expulsion order soon wiped the welcome off the stewardess's face.

'Don't come back Pat', said the one whose uncle had jumped.

'No fucking way', I replied.

# Chapter two

'Bannaher? There's plenty more like him around this town', Larry remarked as we watched the subby heave Jonjo's meagre belongings into the boot of his Mercedes.

'One battered suitcase, not a lot for a lifetime, eh?' Chris rubbed more dirt from our kitchen window as we peered into the street.

'I'd rather starve than work on the fucking buildings again', said Larry as we watched the car pull away.

'Again?' I laughed. 'Refresh my memory'.

'Fuck off, Byrnes. Anyway, working is bad for your health. Look what happened to Jonjo'.

Jonjo had lived in a tiny box room sandwiched between our couple of rooms and the bog. A small, wizened man, his face gleamed like polished leather. The sort of colour I had last seen when my ould fella was soling our shoes in the spare room back home in Croagh.

Jonjo was up and away by six thirty every morning. Hail, rain or snow. Six days a week. He returned around seven every evening, the Evening News, two small bottles of Guinness, and a parcel of food under his arm. He cooked his food in the communal kitchen then retired to his room with his paper and his drink. You could always tell when he was in; his working boots stood on a sheet of newspaper outside his door.

We had got to know him quite well. He told us how he hated the building trade, and the lump system it had spawned. The subby attracted the worst of his criticism; 'work, work, work…that's all he wants. Sticks you down a hole in the morning, and expects it to be an underground car-park in the evening. And pays you nothing at the end of the day…'

'Why do you do it?' I asked him one night.

'Because it's all I know. And it's not as bad as it used to be. When we were building the motorways years ago we lived in camps you wouldn't keep a decent dog in. And you had fellas like Elephant John and Harry the Horse dogging you day and night. Ah, if you could survive that you could survive anything….' Then his voice became hard. 'Besides, it was better than working for those bastards in Lincolnshire'.

He revealed he had emigrated from Leitrim during the war to work on farms in the Lincolnshire area. Many of these farms had been specifically bought by wealthy Englishmen, for their sons, to keep them out of the war. 'The bastards didn't know the first thing about farming, so we were brought in to do the work.

They treated us like dirt; we had to live in stables and haylofts. Working all hours; picking spuds, muck-spreading, harvesting. We had no names; it was Paddy this, Paddy that, Paddy you thick cunt. The prisoners of war were treated better. A year of this slavery was enough for me. I took off for London and got a job with a subby working for McAlpines. I was always looking behind me though...always on the move...'

His conditions of employment required him to report to the local police every three months, otherwise he could be deported. Technically, he was still a fugitive.

'Fuck 'em all', he said to me one evening. 'I'll be fifty next year and I'll have enough put by to get me a little farm near Drumshanbo. And maybe a decent woman to go with it'.

Now he would get neither. Buried alive in the hole he was digging. Three days ago - and nobody missed him. That's how much his departure meant to the world. The absence of his boots had puzzled us a little, but it was only when Bannaher turned up that we learned of his fate. He was arranging for the body to be flown home after the inquest and wanted to send his belongings with it.

'He was too old for this game, anyway', he'd said before he left us. 'Digging is a young man's sport. Do any of yous want a start?'

'A start! Did you hear the bastard?', Larry raged as we watched the Mercedes vanish along the Harrow Road, Jonjo's meagre belongings barely filling the old suitcase now resting on the back seat. 'Jonjo isn't even in his grave yet, and all he can talk about is a start. His kind will bury more than that place over there can hold'.

'That place' was Kensal Green cemetery, which ran parallel with the Harrow Road for some way, and was fronted by a high, ivy-encrusted wall. A wall so grime-ingrained that black might have been its original colour had not the sporadic repairs to the brickwork over the years given the game away.

Not that the view from our front windows bothered us unduly. Dead people were the quietest of neighbours. It was the trains to our rear, rattling our windows at all hours, which had us cursing. The railway embankment sloped up so close in places you could reach out and almost touch them as they rattled by.

'I suppose his next port of call will be Mulligans, telling them all what a great man Jonjo was, before getting some other eejit to take his place'.

We knew Mulligans well. It was one of a litany of pubs we drank our way through. Big and boisterous, it was always packed. It was said you could buy anything there; tax-exemption certificate, dump truck, sticks of dynamite - even a job. You could also cash the likes of Bannaher's cheques. Mulligan was onto a good thing; not only did he get his five percent on the cheques, most of the remainder found its way over the counter too.

Monday mornings at Mulligans were a sight to behold. Bleary-eyed and broke they gathered there; survival the only thing most of them had in common. A day's work would assure them of a sub, and that would tide them over till the next pay-day. Then the sad cycle would begin again. Bannaher and his cronies had them by the balls alright - and they were in no hurry to let go!

-

By now I had been in London for almost a year, and very little of that time had been devoted to work. There were occasional early-morning forays to Mulligans when funds were low, but generally, signing on at a couple of Labour Exchanges, using Fergus' name at one of them, brought in a steady income. Well…what Fergus didn't know wouldn't bother him…

Catching the eye of a subby in the early-morning fog wasn't too difficult; some of the hopefuls looked as if they might struggle to lift a pint never mind a pick and shovel. The mystery tour we called it; you never knew where you would wind up once you plonked your arse in the back of that Transit van. One day you might be digging holes all over Watford, the next pulling cables outside Birmingham. Better than pulling you wire all day, Chris was fond of saying. Only just, boy. Only just.

Larrry never took part. The time of the first race usually dictated what time he got out of bed. If he wasn't in the betting shops trying to relieve William Hill of some money he was dreaming up ways of relieving shopkeepers and other business people of their hard-earned cash.

The three of us had drifted together in the way that casual acquaintances tend to after a while. The group was fluid by nature, the faces constantly changing, but retaining a nucleus of half a dozen or so. Chris and Larry shared a double room in a rundown house off the Kilburn High Road and had secured a basement room for me. It had a picture of a tropical island painted on the front wall in place of a window, and a permanent smell of stale cabbage and greasy pans lingered in the air. McGinty, the landlord, appeared once a week to collect his rent, ignoring the fact that his pride and joy was falling down around us, complaining that he couldn't afford repairs on the money he was charging. We decided to get out before they had to dig us out; hence our arrival in Kensal Green.

16

Chris, Larry and me, three friends with little in common except our gambling and thieving. There was our Irishness of course; though Chris reckoned he was London-born. He had spent his first couple of years in the East End until his mother had tired of his father's beatings and left him. She had kept his step-sister and sent him to an aunt in Limerick. He had remained in ignorance of his true identity until the aunt confessed on her death-bed. He was seventeen at the time. Within a week he had stolen fifty three pounds from the local creamery and fled to London.

Larry had originated in the Ringsend area of Dublin. His mother still lived there and he visited her occasionally. These visits were very secretive, and I suspected there was a warrant out for him on some charge or other.

As for me, my story wasn't much better. Ever since I could remember, I was a rebel. As Fr Maguire put it the night I tried to burn the school down; 'that young man is going places, all the wrong ones'. Since being kicked out of school I had tried a variety of jobs, and had being kicked out of most of them. By this time my father had given up on me. His only comment when he found out I was headed for London was 'good riddance'. Mother cried and gave me ten pounds, a bottle of holy water and a picture of Blessed Martin. Fergus had chipped in with another tenner.

Living in London hardened me. Work became a dirty word - the only kind of work I was qualified for anyhow. I saw what too many days down damp holes had done to scores of my countrymen. You only had to walk down the Kilburn High Road or Cricklewood Broadway to witness it. In the cafes and pubs, in the clubs, in dingy little rooms that passed for home, old and bent before their time. And nothing to show for it; all pissed up against the pub walls or left in the clubs and betting shops.

I grew to hate the sight of a pick and shovel. Hate the blistered hands and the aching back, the company of loud-mouthed navvies with their passion for the pub at the end of every shift. Beery evenings in damp and mud-caked clothes, then back to a squalid room in a squalid house to consume pie and chips…Jaysus, it was the stuff of nightmares. To contemplate doing it for the rest of my life….

'This town is full of Jonjos', I said as we downed a few pints of the black stuff in his memory. Naturally, the venue was Mulligans. Mulligan himself was behind the bar on this occasion, lining up pints with all the finesse of an orangutan.

'Look at that ape', said Larry. 'He'd look more at home shoveling shit in a slurry pit. A bog man right up to his eyebrows'.

'You can take the man from the bog but you can't take the bog from the man', said Chris.

Mulligan hailed from the wilds of Kerry, Killorglin I believe, and was famous in a minor sort of way. He had once been a strongman in Duffy's Circus, and toured Ireland performing feats of strength. Later, he attracted a lot of publicity at shows all over England, pulling buses with the tow-rope held between his teeth, and taking on - and beating - tractors in tug-o-war contests. Or so the legend had it.

He flexed his muscles now as he placed our drinks in front of us.

'What do you think, lads? Fifty next birthday - and still fit as a fiddle'.

'Jonjo would have been fifty next birthday, too', I replied.

'Is that a fact? Ah, poor fella. God rest him'. He blessed himself. 'He didn't come in here much. Only the weekend, to change his cheque. He wasn't a one for the diesel'.

No he wasn't. Not that there was any shortage of those, I thought, looking around. Some of those here could do without clothes, without food, without women: the one thing they couldn't do without was drink. The diesel. I remembered Jonjo's words to me once; 'I like a drop of the diesel, Terry boy, but only now and again. Isn't the craving an awful affliction? I do see men in the morning and they on fire for a sup of the craythur. That fire do be burning all their lives; it's what keeps them down their damp holes, and in their squalid little rooms, their dream of going home just that - dreams. There's men I know haven't been home for twenty years. They'll never go back now, or if they do it'll be the one-way ride in the ould pine box. And many of them won't even afford that'.

'No, he wasn't one for the diesel'...Mulligan was still talking. 'Not like yourselves, eh? Still, it's an ill wind. Mind you...' He lowered his voice an octave and looked over to where Bannaher was holding court...'I heartell it was all getting too much for him. Couldn't pull the socks off a dead man anymore...' He shook his head and moved away to serve someone else.

'You wait', Larry raged, 'before the week is out, they'll have him dying of natural causes'.

'Or committing suicide'.

The swing doors to our right crashed open as Chris spoke. A wild-eyed barrel of a man swayed in the opening momentarily, then stepped inside. His red beard contrasted sharply with the darker hair on his head. There was a momentary silence then Bannaher stepped forward and tried to urge the newcomer towards the group. The other man shrugged the guiding hand away, and there ensued a heated discussion, although in voices quiet enough to prevent them being overheard.

'Duggan', said Larry. 'Tanked up as usual'.

Mick Duggan. Dougie to most of us who knew him, was a one-man demolition gang who demolished buildings that were only one step away from falling down. Big Bertha, a fourteen-pound sledgehammer, was his favourite tool; he wielded it like a cutlass, scaling structures that lesser mortals feared to tread, and flattening them with his mighty swipes. Who needed a wrecking ball when you had Dougie! Besides, he was a lot cheaper. Bannaher was currently using him to flatten a street of terraced shacks to the rear of Willesden Lane.

Whatever the dispute between the two men was, it was quickly settled. Bannaher took a wallet from his pocket and passed some notes to Dougie, then patted him on the arm before returning to the group.

Dougie weaved his way in our direction, calling for a pint, before turning to us.

'The three musketeers themselves! Well now, we don't see much of you at the pick-and- shovel saloon these mornings'.

'Ah no, we've given it up', I replied. 'It's bad for your health'.

'It was for Jonjo's anyway'. This was Larry.

'And what would you know about work? About as much as my arse knows about snipe-shooting'.

He drank deeply, almost half emptying his glass before replacing it on the counter. 'He was packing it in, you know. A few more months. Goin' back home in style, he said'. He gave a dry laugh. 'Some style now, eh?' The pint was raised to his lips again. 'I could have saved him'. A pause. 'I should have saved him'.

'You were there?'

'I was there, boy. Saw the whole thing. From the roof of the old school across the way. He was digging out around the footings of an old wall when the whole lot went in on top of him. Ah Christ, it took me five minutes to get to him - when it should'a taken two'. He waved the pint. 'Too much of this, I suppose. That, and the fact that I tripped over something and nearly broke me fucking neck. Anyway, when I got there it was too late'. He shook his head. 'He shouldn't have been down there at all. There wasn't a bit of shuttering to be seen'.

'Since when did the likes of Bannaher let a little matter like that bother him?' This was Larry again. 'Everyone around Cricklewood knows **his** slogan; 'I'm paying you to dig holes not put up shuttering''.

Dougie's grip on his glass tightened.

'I wouldn't go repeating that if I was you…'

'No, you wouldn't. But then, I don't work for the bastard'. His glass banged on the counter. 'Come on lads, there's a bad smell in here - and it isn't the drink'.

A few days later, none of us were very surprised when the inquest returned a verdict of death by misadventure.

# Chapter three

'Meet Tessa - my new partner', said Chris as I entered the living room.

'I already have', I shouted. 'She stole my bloody wallet'.

It was barely an hour since our first meeting. The venue had been the Banba Club, at the tea-dance, where hung-over Irishmen sobered up on a Sunday afternoon, waiting for the pubs to re-open. Situated up an alleyway off the Kilburn High Road, it was a low-roofed shack of a building, and had probably once seen service as stables. Some of the locals were of the opinion that it still catered for animals.

The afternoon had been a little more eventful than usual; apart from the removal of my wallet and the mandatory couple of fights, The Sunshine Gang had paid one of their occasional visits. They had, as usual, been repelled. But not before they had wedged a Mini in the entrance, busted a doorman's nose, and smashed the window to the ticket office. In the fighting that had ensued, sheer numbers had driven them back into the street. They had retreated, vowing revenge. I had landed a punch on a greasy head and had returned to the mineral bar feeling pleased with myself.

The dance that followed was a Siege of Ennis, and I found myself dragged into the mass of gyrating bodies by Tessa. She stood out among the other dancers; tall and athletic- looking, ash-blonde hair billowing out behind her as she jigged - inexpertly - to the music. I managed to hang on to her for the following slow waltz, and discovered that it was her first time to an Irish dance. Afterwards, she disappeared to wherever it is women go to when dances are over. A few minutes later I discovered my wallet had disappeared too.

'No hard feeling, Terry?' She handed me back the wallet, a big grin on her face. 'It wasn't my idea'.

'I know it wasn't'. I extracted a fiver and handed it to Chris. 'You proved your point'.

'I told you she was good'. He laughed and clapped me on the back.

Chris' pick -and-shovel days were over. His weekly ten-shilling accumulator on the ITV Seven had finally come good: from his winnings he had purchased a new suit and shoes, and became a pickpocket in the West End. Tessa was his latest assistant.

Tessa lit up a cigarette then offered them round. 'Is that what you call a dance in Ireland?

Chris laughed. 'It was a bit lively, I suppose'.

'Who, exactly, is The Sunshine Gang?'

Larry raised his head from The Sporting Chronicle. 'A bunch of bowsies from back yonder'. Where yonder was he didn't specify. 'We had the right treatment for them in Ringsend'.

'We Know. The ould Ringsend uppercut', I chuckled, having heard it all before.

'And what is a Ringsend uppercut?', she asked

'A good kick in the...' Larry hesitated,...'whats-its'.

Chris nudged Tessa. 'Larry used to run with them, didn't you?'

'From a distance, boy. Only from a distance'. He snorted. 'They came over here to lick their wounds'.

Despite Larry's low opinion of them, they had already acquired a reputation in the area, and when fights broke out in the dancehalls and clubs they were usually in the thick of it.

The arrival of Tessa changed our lives quite a lot. I had never met anyone quite like her before. She wasn't the first liberated woman I had come in to contact with, but she was different. Certainly different from the Irish girls you met at the dances in the Galtymore and the 32 Club. Oh, you could shift them, but no matter how much drink you poured down their gullets, all you were likely to get at the end of the night was a good feel. And sometimes not even that. Getting your leg over meant putting a roof over their heads. Marriages might be made in heaven but they were negotiated in dancehalls like the Galtymore.

They worked like beavers in the sweatshops of Kilburn and Cricklewood. At Smiths and Walls, Heinz and Unigate, from eight till five, then hurried away to supplement their meagre wages by doing evening shifts as usherettes and assemblers in the cinemas and factories. Weekends they prowled the dancehalls looking for husbands - men who would be content with a furtive fumble in the back of a Mini or Austin 1100, and who could be weaned off the Guinness without too much fuss. Oh yes, behind every drunken Irishman was a sober Irish girl.

Into this came Tessa like a breath of fresh air. Twiggy, Jean Shrimpton, songs of peace, rioting students, she scorned all that. She was a materialist, out, as she put it, to screw the world before it screwed her. There was no such thing as free love.

'There's a price for everything', she said, 'especially love'.

'Why a pickpocket?', I asked her one evening.

'Why not? It's better than a bleedin' factory. I left school at fifteen, home at sixteen. I got cheesed off being pawed by my dad - step-dad actually - and my mum couldn't give a toss. Too busy doing the amusement arcades by day and her bingo at night. My brother Ben was nicking cars for a living - when he wasn't inside. I just took off one day. I don't think anybody missed me'.

One afternoon she turned up at the flat, limping. She asked me to fetch some ice-cubes, then explained she had fallen down some steps on the Embankment.

'Stupid, really. I wasn't watching where I was going and tripped over. I had the stuff Chris passed to me in my bag. It could have been serious, I guess...'

'Maybe it's an omen'.

She laughed. 'If you believe all that crap. My mum believes in black cats, not walking under ladders, throwing salt over your left shoulder, all that stuff, and it hasn't brought her much luck. I believe you make your own'.

Her skirt had ridden up and I could see her knickers. Black, lacy affairs. Go on, something kept telling me, she wouldn't let you see the view if she didn't want you to do something about it. However, before I could act, the door opened and Chris walked in.

My drift into crime probably began with that incident, because next day I was standing in for her as Chris's assistant. And very boring it was too. I spent my time sauntering up and down a stretch of Piccadilly while he searched for suitable victims. At the end of the day we had acquired a purse with everything in it except money, a wallet containing five one pound notes, a train ticket to Hemel Hempstead, and a photo of a nude woman with 'I love you, Dicko' scrawled across it. Our other acquisition confirmed my suspicions that the English were sex-mad; a gold-embossed cigarette case with ten French ticklers packed neatly inside. We shared the condoms and pawned the case for eight quid. Not exactly a fortune for a day's work. Chris said there were better days, but I didn't really fancy it. I was glad when Tessa recovered.

Since Jonjo's death I hadn't taken a pick or shovel in my hand. And I had no intention of doing so. London was a goldmine, waiting to be exploited. Larry was right; it was a great place for those with no intention of getting up in the morning. We began stealing on a small scale, and found the Portobello market on a Saturday morning very obliging. It was incredibly easy; hiding the gear in special pockets inside our long coats. Jeans and shirts were the easiest to flog in the pubs we hawked them round. We extended our operations to take in other markets; Petticoat Lane and Brick Lane, and found that shops like Burtons and Colliers were just as obliging.

By now I had acquired Larry's passion for the horses. Sometimes it seemed as if I was stealing for William Hills or Terry Downes; come late afternoon, the money I'd made in the morning had vanished behind the counter of a dingy betting shop in Willesden Lane or Kilburn High Road. Other times we were rolling in it; like when Saucy Kit won the Champion Hurdle and Fleet the One Thousand Guineas, and we had them doubled up to win hundreds of pounds. We followed up on Royal Palace in the Two Thousand Guineas and The Derby.

It was Tessa who suggested the break in Brighton when she saw us counting our winnings after the Derby. Larry wouldn't come - he had bought a small van for fifty pounds and wanted to practice his driving - so Chris, Tessa and myself headed off.

I still couldn't figure Tessa out. For several months now she had graced us with her presence, but she was as enigmatic as ever. One thing was clear though; she wasn't Chris's girlfriend, merely his working partner. She was even vague about where she lived; over Walthamstow way was the nearest I could pin her down to, and if Chris knew he wasn't saying. Sometimes we wouldn't see her for a week or more, and apart from occasional outing to the pub with us, where she downed pints of lager without ever seeming to get pissed, her social life was a total mystery. I badly wanted to get inside her knickers, and it was frustrating watching her parade her talents round the flat when I couldn't seem to get close to her.

Brighton changed all that. We were like kids again at the seaside. We built sandcastles, raced each other along the beach, got sick on jellied eels. And even sicker on beer. We had taken sleeping bags with us, sleeping huddled together beneath the promenade for the first few nights. Then Chris met an old friend, and she dragged him off to the Isle of Wight to some concert she had tickets for. I was fed up of sleeping on lumpy terrain, so I suggested we book into a couple of hotel rooms that night.

.'Make it a double', she replied.

Making love with her was like being aboard a runaway train. A hair-raising ride, constantly picking up speed, gathering momentum. I wondered if we were ever going to stop. On and on we rode, free-wheeling in places, generating sparks galore where the friction was fiercest. Eventually, we coasted to a stop on an uphill section. Out of steam. Well, I was anyway. Her body in repose was the nearest thing to a work of art I had ever seen. Long flanks perfectly aligned, breasts sculpted out of the finest, palest clay; nostrils flared, lips slightly parted as she slumbered.

Sunrise found us on the beach again, watching the sun clamber over the horizon. I knew how it felt.

It was then that she asked me for a hundred pounds.

'It's for my mum. To stop the bailiffs givin' her the heave-ho. Dad's done a runner again and Ben's in the nick...'

'It's a lot of dosh'.

She shrugged. 'It's only money, Terry. Bits of paper. Easy come, easy go. Besides, you'll only lose it all again. You always do'. She rubbed a hand along the inside of my thigh. 'Think of it as a long-term investment'.

I couldn't figure out what she was offering me; love, friendship, or merely the use of her body. Whatever it was, I wanted it. I gave her the hundred quid. When we got back to London Bridge she kissed me goodbye and said she would see me soon.

'Where's Tessa?' Larry asked when he saw me on my own.

'You guess is as good as mine. She borrowed some money then took off'.

He looked at me in peculiar fashion. 'She borrowed some off me too. Before ye left. For her brother's bail, she said'.

I gave him a highly selective version of our exploits, omitting any reference to our steamy session in the hotel. That was our secret. Something to be savoured in moments of solitude. Not an item to be tossed casually into the conversation as if it were about a football match or a horse race. Some of the girls we tangled with were fair game, but this was something different.

Besides, I had seen the way Larry looked at her.

Chris turned up later the evening complaining of a wasted journey.

''She was on the rags. All I got was a couple of hand jobs. I could have done that myself. Besides, she got me there under false pretences. Said Bob Dylan was goin' to be playing...'

'And he wasn't?'

'Naw. It was that fucking Donovan...' He began to sing. 'They call me mellow yellow... what a wanker'.

He didn't seem surprised to hear about the money. 'Did she say what for?'

For her mother...or brother'. Larry gave him the details.

Chris laughed. 'Not her brother. She hasn't got one. Least, not called Ben'.

'How come you know so much about her all of a sudden?' I said, annoyed now that I had ever mentioned the money.

He shrugged. 'Little things I picked up. You can't spend time with people and not learn something. Human nature, isn't it?'. He grinned. 'I suppose I'd better start looking for a new partner…'

# Chapter four

When Larry wasn't stuck in the racing pages, he was plotting new ways of making money. We knew we were petty thieves - small fry in the world of crime - but, as, we kept telling ourselves, it was better than working for a living. Anyway, we could dream, couldn't we? Today, knocking off market stalls; tomorrow the Great Train Robbery!

Lock-up premises became our specialty, and the railway line that ran behind our house was very convenient for the places we set out to rob. It traversed the Harrow Road and snaked round Scrubs Lane, where there were plenty of warehouses and factories suited to our purpose. We only selected places that had no night watchman; not that we felt cowardly or anything, but we didn't want the added complication of assault included in our armoury. For one thing, it got the police more interested. For another, it was property we wanted to hit not people.

Between nine and eleven at night was the best time to be about our business; it was late enough for the premises to be empty, but not late enough to arouse the suspicions of the police if they spotted you in the vicinity.

Our initial efforts were purely speculative; taking what we hoped we could sell; typewriters, adding machines, offices chairs etc. These we lugged along the railway line, scampering up the embankment whenever a train was heard approaching. The following day we loaded them into Larry's van, selling them to a guy that operated a second-hand office furniture business from a railway arch near Queens Park station.

Once, we broke into the lock-up petrol station along the Harrow Road from us, Larry being convinced that the takings were locked away in a filing cabinet every night. It backed onto the railway, so it was chicken feed to jemmy the back door open. We searched in vain for the money; all we found in the cabinet was lots of blank Green Shield books - and hundreds of sheets of stamps. We took the lot with us, then spent most of the night licking and sticking - something which Chris thought hilarious. Still, we managed to raise about thirty quid for our efforts.

Larry was mechanical- minded and liked messing about with old record players and other gadgets, repairing them then selling them on. He even rebuilt a juke-box once, and had it installed in the nearby café that we used, splitting the proceeds with the owner. Then he got hold of a high-powered air pistol, which he adapted to fire ball-bearings. Afterwards, we took a trip to the dump, found some old plate glass and tried it out. I was amazed at the results; a neat hole in the glass every time.

Armed with this contraption, we ventured out in the van in the evenings, seeking suitable lock-up jewelers. After we'd located one, we parked close by, and having made sure the street was clear, fired at the jeweler's window through a hole we had made in the side of the van. The resultant hole in the glass was large enough to enable us to fish out small items of jewelery using a length of coat-hanger wire. We sold the proceeds from a briefcase down the Portobello Market on Saturday mornings, one of us keeping a sharp look-out for the law.

Ironically, the closest we came to the police was when a couple of thieving bastards snatched the briefcase and legged it in the direction of Ladbroke Grove. A nearby stall-holder gave chase, and somebody else went searching for a copper. We decided that discretion was the better part of valour and made ourselves scarce.

The operation gradually fizzled out, partly because of the publicity it received, but mainly due to technological advances. The new trembler alarms tended to go off if you as much as looked at them, and after we'd set a few of them ringing we decided to call it a day.

We got into the habit of frequenting the Ace café, an all-night dive that was more than an eating house for many who used it. It was a meeting place, a way of life, perhaps even a home for some. It looked as if it had fallen off the back of some passing lorry and had landed lopsidedly on the edge of the North Circular Road, near Stonebridge Park station. There it sat, its neon sign blazing, the jukebox blasting, attracting the flotsam and jetsam of the city just as easily as it absorbed the grime from the passing traffic

Inside, there were bikers, long-distance lorry drivers, small-time villains like ourselves, probably a few hookers, definitely a sprinkling of people of no fixed abode. Sometimes, we sat there drinking strong coffee, playing sad songs on the jukebox. And watching all the lonesome faces as 'Take These Chains From My Heart' and 'Are You Lonesome Tonight?' permeated the fried-bacon and dog-roll atmosphere. Some nights Eleanor Rigby turned up, pushing her worldly goods before her in a battered pram. We called her Eleanor because she said John Lennon had seen her there one night and written the song for her. She was about sixty, lived in a steel container near Wembley Stadium, and nearly always sported two bright red slashes of lipstick that never quite lined up with her lips. She invariably sang along in a high screeching voice whenever someone played the record on the jukebox;

'All the lonely people / where do they all come from
All the lonely people / where do they all belong'
'The Beatles in the Ace?' said Larry. 'I fucking doubt it'.
Looking around me, I wasn't so sure.

A lot of our scheming and planning took place in the Ace. Although our crimes were small our ambitions weren't. We were merely practising for now; building up to the day when we would really make it big. Nothing too spectacular; some swindle or con that would net us ten grand or so would do nicely.

Chris, meantime, was making great strides. Unable to find anyone to replace Tessa - who hadn't been seen for a few weeks - he had abandoned his small removals business for larger removals. Anyway, as he himself put it; 'there's so many dips in the West End now we're picking each others' pockets'. Instead, he had hired a couple of lock-up garages and was filling them with fridges, washing machines, TV's and other household goods that he got from High-Street stores on the never-never. They were falling over themselves, selling him stuff he was never- never going to pay for!

I couldn't believe it was so easy.

Chris laughed and patted his immaculate suit (another purchase on the never-never).

'The whistle is half the battle. As far as they're concerned I'm a man of property. If you can convince them you've got bricks and mortar, credit is no problem'.

It was a beautiful scheme. He viewed empty houses on the pretext of buying them, got duplicate keys cut then convinced the stores he was the owner and had the goods delivered there. As soon as the delivery van disappeared around the corner, we whisked the gear away to safety in Larry's van. Chris then sold the items through a network of local newspapers.

There was still no word from Tessa, though Chris said she would be back. In the meantime, he had taken up with Bernie, a dark-haired girl he had picked up in the Galtymore dance hall one night. At first he was all over her; she was one of the few Irish girls to open her legs without preconditions, he said. Cozy nights in the double room she shared with her friend Annie, where she fed him plates of pork chops and mashed potatoes, eventually convinced him she was after more than his body. 'There's wedding bells ringing in her head', he said one night when she was ringing our doorbell'. 'Tell her I'm not in'.

After that he took to avoiding her, although she was always good for an occasional night when he was stuck. It took a long time to sink in that he was avoiding her. Then one night I opened the door to her. I could tell she had been drinking.

'Tell that bastard he can't treat me like a piece of dirt'. She pushed past me. 'Never mind, I'll tell him myself'.

'He's not here, Bernie', I said as she staggered into his room and threw herself on the bed. 'He won't be back till tomorrow'.

''I'll wait'. She closed her eyes, spread her hands wide and began to breathe deeply.

Chris and Larry had gone to Birmingham to flog some washing machines and fridges and were staying overnight so it looked like I was stuck with her. I left her to her own devices, went out and had a few pints, then went to bed, forgetting all about her. In the middle of the night she woke me up.

'It's freezing out there, Terry. Can I come in with you?' She climbed in and began to fondle me. However, when I got her knickers off she seemed to go into some kind of paralysis and lay there immobile while I tried to enter her. In the end I gave up, rolled over and had a quiet wank and went to sleep. When I awoke in the morning she had gone.

Towards the end of autumn Fergus came over for a week's holiday. His arrival wasn't unexpected; mother was a great one for letter-writing and had forewarned me. Her letters were like serials, each one picking up where the last one left off, and each one packed with the minutiae of life back home. It was if she feared I might forget all about them if she didn't put it all down on paper.

'Stand back and let the dog see the rabbit!,' Fergus shouted when he saw me. The intervening years hadn't changed him much - apart from the bushy beard now covering his face. It suited him I thought; it gave prominence to his rather demonic eyes. Always the joker, his impish sense of humour was constantly mirrored in those twinkling, roguish blue eyes. He was six years older than me, and I had idolised him when I was growing up.

The news from home was much as I expected; mother worrying about me, father silent and autocratic as always. Fergus was still working on Costello's stud farm, a few miles the other side of Croagh.

'I remember a conversation with you a long time ago', I said to him the first evening. 'You told me it was your ambition to own your own stud farm some day. 'Give me ten years', you said, 'and I'll have it made'. I hate to jog your memory, big brother, but your ten years is up'.

He laughed. 'And I seem to recall you telling me you were going to be a big game hunter in Africa. Childish dreams Terry boy…childish dreams'. He paused. 'Times are bad, boy. So bad that I'm thinking of trading my stirrups for a pick and shovel'. Another pause; 'Costello has taken to training a few of his own to make ends meet'.

Costello: gentleman farmer and breeder of thoroughbred horses as a hobby. His main livelihood was derived from the breeding and exporting thoroughbred bulls to clients mostly from the Middle East. The biggest bull-shipper in Ireland, was how he liked to describe himself.

I remembered the farm from childhood; the smart spick-and span buildings that housed the animals contrasted sharply with his own living quarters. This was a kind of granny-flat that had been tacked on to the gable-end of the large, rambling house that had lain empty ever since his mother had died. He was the last of that particular Costello strain; an only son who had never married, and his refusal to live in the old house had to do with the fact that it was now haunted. At least, that was what he believed.

I had spent many occasions standing on my tiptoes, peering through the cobwebbed windows, hoping for a glimpse of the ghost, said to be that of his mother. All I ever saw was old furniture gone mildewed with age, dust-covered ornaments and pictures, and a tall grandfather clock that ticked no more.

His own quarters had all the hallmarks of being squatted in; piles of old papers and magazines, clothes and cooking utensils scattered about, and jars and bottles covered in cobwebs littering tables and shelves. Fergus used to say that his animals lived better than he did.

I never gave a thought to how odd he was. I was more interested in the money he generally gave to me. He had jars brimming with coins; coins on the mantle-piece, coins on the dresser, and when I was around he usually pressed a few into my palm. I had always thought of him as being so rich he didn't have to show it (or look it). And now he was having to race a few of his horses to make a living.

'I wouldn't have thought it worth his while', I said. 'The prize money would hardly keep him in cigars. Not those bloody great things he smokes anyhow!'.

Fergus laughed. 'It's not the prize money he's after. It the bookies money'. Then he told me that Hourigan, the local bookie, had been cleaned out. 'He was only playing at it, anyway. No real money behind him. Costello turned him over with a couple of well-laid out ones at Mallow. Cost him thousands 'cos he never laid any of it off'. Another laugh. 'Talk about unlucky! If he was an undertaker people would stop dying'.

He sounded stupid to me, not unlucky.

The week turned out to be a hard-drinking one. We pub-crawled from Cricklewood to Harlesden, then back again. Several times. The Rising Sun, The Case Is Altered, The Green Man, The Spotted Dog, we got thrown out of all of them. We didn't mind; weren't we enjoying ourselves!

Bernie and some of her friends were roped in to help with the enjoyment. Most of them worked in the Radiomobile factory in Neasden, 'soldering knobs on radios', as Bernie put it, or 'polishing bedpans in Dollis Hill' - a reference to the hospital there, where some of them worked as student nurses.

Bernie never referred to our abortive attempt at sex it my bed. Nor did I mention it at our next encounter - in the back of Larry's van on our way to the Buffalo Club in Camden Town. Her on/off relationship with Chris was on at the moment and it didn't seem appropriate. Fergus nearly didn't get into the club as he wasn't wearing a tie - an oversight that was corrected when the doorman sold him one from a box of them he had conveniently at hand. The fact that it was bright green and completely at odds with his sober blue blazer didn't worry Fergus. He was getting on great guns with Annie. 'She can solder my knob any time she likes', he informed me in the gents, so I left them to it.

Later, at the bar, we bumped into Mick Duggan. He was holding himself together in the casual manner of people who are drunker than they think. Fergus slapped him on the shoulder.

'You can let go of the bar, Dougie. You're not on the high seas now'.

Dougie let out a whoop. I had forgotten they had gone to school together, and had gained a sort of notoriety when, along with several others, they had barricaded our sadistic headmaster in the classroom one day and kicked the shit out of him.

'No, I'm on the high stool you hairy ould bollix'. He shook Fergus's hand vigorously, then tugged playfully at his beard. 'Snap'. The words came out slurred. 'I'm always on the high stool these days'.

'Ah, what can't be cured must be endured...'

'No, I mean it. A drunken bum, that's me'. He flexed his muscles. 'Look at me! There was a time when I could pull a house down with these hands. Now I couldn't pull me wire...' He began to sing:

I'm a rambler, I'm a gambler, I'm a long way from home
And if you don't like me well leave me alone

32

I'll eat when I'm hungry, I'll drink when I'm dry

And if moonshine don't kill me I'll live till I die.

Later, we all returned to a wild nurses' party in Dollis Hill. It was Fergus' last night in London and he made the most of it, because the last I saw of him he was heading down a corridor with Annie hanging off him. I got so drunk I fell asleep on a table in the communal lounge, and was still there when the cleaning women came round. Dougie was discovered hours later, unconscious in a broom cupboard.

Fergus wasn't taken in by me. He knew I was living a peculiar sort of life.

'Don't go breaking your mother's heart any more than you have already done', were his parting words to me.

I didn't know it, but it was the last time I would ever see him again.

-

One night, in the Ace, Larry got picked up by a handsome-looking woman who must have been well into her forties. (That was a thing with Larry - he liked older women)

''I'm well in there, lads', he said the following day. 'Her old man died a few months back and left her a big house in Willesden Green. And loads of money as well'.

'He must have been a subby then', said Chris.

We didn't see a lot of him for the next week, until one morning he turned up in a suit several sizes too big for him, and wearing carpet slippers. The clothes belonged to his lady-friend's dead husband, and were all he could get his hands on when making his bid for freedom.

'I know now what killed him', he said. 'She wanted it all the fucking time. D'you know what she did? Hid my clothes to stop me leaving'. He put on a lady's voice; 'One more time and you can have your trousers back, Laurence', He shook his head. 'Ah Jasus, she's sex mad'. He shook the oversize coat. 'As soon as she went to the bog this morning I grabbed this suit and took off'.

The incident kept him away from the Ace for a while, and she made several enquires of Chris and myself as to where he had gone. We told her he had gone to America.

'Oh, she said, clearly disappointed. 'There are some…items of his at my place. Would one of you care to call round and collect them?'

.No thank you!', we both chorused.

We gave the suit to a regular, who we had christened the Michelin Man. His eyes were practically invisible, he wore a mouthful of false teeth, and he carried a plastic bag of vomit around with him, The vomit was food - usually from the café - that he had regurgitated. Apparently, he had an ulcer problem, causing him to puke up the food. We reckoned he took it home and ate it again. A few nights after we gave him the suit we saw our lady friend giving him funny looks as he puked into his bag.

It was through an acquaintance met in the Ace that we had our first real brush with the law. Our air-gun was redundant by now, and we were desperately seeking new ways of increasing our cash-flow.

'Allie?' remarked the acquaintance, when the name of a certain shopkeeper kept cropping up, 'he's the biggest fence around. Cigarettes now, he'll take all you can supply and no questions asked'.

This was good enough for us. We soon established our bona-fides and he agreed to pay us half the retail price for everything we brought him.

We had already decided on a target; a lock-up newsagents in nearby Wembley. It was alarmed, but it was an external bell type, which was easy to neutralise, merely a matter of sticking a piece of cardboard between the gong and the mechanism. I accomplished this from the roof of Larry's van then we made short work of the door with a crowbar.

We reckoned it to be a quick in-and-out job; no more than a couple of minutes to grab what cartons and loose packets we could find. We were almost finished when the alarm went off like an air-raid siren.

'Jesus!', roared Larry, 'the fucken' cardboard's fell out'.

Soon there were lights coming on everywhere, and voices shouting. Worse, a vicious-sounding dog started a racket a few doors away.

It was time to go. We piled head-first into the van; I managed to pull a blanket over the evidence and we had regained some semblance of composure as we turned into Wembley High Road. It was then that the Panda car pulled in behind us and began to keep pace with us. Not knowing what else to do, I just kept driving. And the Panda kept following.

I nudged Larry. 'What do we do?'

Larry seemed to have lost the power of speech, apart from mumbling incoherently.

'This is no time for fucken' praying', I shouted. I did some quick calculations; no tax, no insurance, no driving licence…all that gear in the back. We were up shit creek.

I gave Larry a kick in the shins. 'I'm baling out the next red lights. You'd better do the same if you don't want to spend the next few birthdays in nick'.

34

I guess we timed it right. As we ejected at the lights the cops were also getting out, putting their caps on. I could hear their shouts as I leaped a hedge and hared off across a stretch of parkland. I was young and fit and easily lost my pursuers. Trouble was, I got lost myself in the process, and not wishing to show myself on the streets in case the cops were still on the prowl, I decided to kip under some bushes until daylight.

I was stiff, sore and soaked to the bone when I finally made it back to the flat. Larry was sound asleep in his bed. He had encountered no problems, having come across a bicycle in a nearby driveway, and was indoors within fifteen minutes of taking to his heels.

We never discovered what happened to the van or its contents, and the experience put the wind up us for some time after that. Still, you can't keep good men down. Within a week Larry had a new set of wheels - a Triumph Herald, white with a black sun roof.

'What d'you reckon?', he asked after he had driven it away from the garage. 'Fifty down and twenty quid a month'.

I laughed. 'I reckon not many instalments will get paid'.

I was right. Within a couple of months the finance company was round trying to re-possess it. And not having much luck. The first time they called they found it chained to a tree. Larry took to keeping it in a garage after that. On a subsequent visit they came armed with a pair of bolt cutters. We took great delight in telling them that both Larry and the car had gone on a long visit to Ireland.

## Chapter five

Tessa's return was as bizarre as it was unexpected. More than four months had passed without a word from her. A lifetime it seemed to me, and I had convinced myself I would never see her again. Chris never had any doubts; 'She'll be back one of these days, wait and see...'

She appeared at the Ace one night with a truck driver who looked as if he spent more time under his truck than driving it.

'Thanks for nothing!' she shouted as she preceded him. 'Give a girl a lift and you think that's it. I'd rather sleep in a ditch...'

Chris stuck out a leg as the driver went by.

'You heard what she said...'

Tessa hadn't seen us, and as she turned round the driver picked himself up, grabbed a sauce bottle and lunged in our direction. Two things happened almost simultaneously; one of the bikers seated nearby grabbed his arm and stopped him in his tracks, and Tessa attacked him from the rear. She kicked him hard between the legs. He let out a howl and dropped to the floor again.

That ended the fight but not the excitement. A few moments later - in the midst of the bikers raucous celebrations - I heard a horrific rending noise coming from the car park.

'He wasn't much of a fighter, was he?', one of the bikers said to me.

'No, and he isn't much of a driver either', I replied. 'He's just run over your bikes'.

Several of us piled into the Triumph and chased him along the North Circular, but we lost him the other side of Hendon.

Where did you pick him up?' I asked Tessa when things had quietened down.

'D'you mind! He picked me up - outside Birmingham. God, it was freezing in that lay-by'.

What were you doing in a lay-by outside Birmingham? Where were you coming from?' This was from Larry.

'Manchester. What a dump! I couldn't stand it there any longer'. She saw that an explanation was called for. 'That's where I've been. With me mum. The threat of eviction was making her ill, so when a friend offered her a place in Manchester she took it. I went with her to help her settle in'.

'And Ben, did he go too?'

I saw something flash between Chris and her, but Larry didn't seem to notice.

'I shouldn't have lied to you. I'm sorry. It was a spur of the moment thing…but I needed money badly…'

'You could have told me the truth'.

She stood up. 'If it's your bloody money you're worried about, you'll get it back…' She picked up her hold-all.

Chris put out his hand. 'It's the middle of the night. Where are you going?' She shrugged.

'You can stay with us'. Larry didn't object. She sat down again.

Looking at her, I realised how much I had missed her. There was something about her - I couldn't put my finger on what it was - that got to me. The girls that had kept me company - and there had been a few since her departure - faded into insignificance when she was around.

She looked different now. Her hair had been cropped short, and there were large crescent ear-rings dangling from her lobes. Gold by the look of them. The three-quarter length leather jacket she was wearing also suggested she was something less than poverty-stricken.

She hadn't wasted her time in Manchester. She was going into business, she told us.

'Jewelery'…'

Her mother's friend owned a string of cheap jewelery kiosks throughout the city. Located mostly in the new shopping centres that were springing up, and he was cleaning up. When he saw her interest, he offered to supply her with all his lines on a sale-or-return basis. He even suggested she try out a few markets first to see how she got on.

'To be honest, I think he was only trying to get rid of me'. She laughed. 'Him and me mum were, you know… Anyway, I think it's a great idea. I can get the stuff dirt-cheap and charge London prices…'

She was on a winner straight away. The first Saturday morning, in Bell Street market, she sold out. She doubled her order and sold that the following Saturday. She realised she had struck gold. Within a short time she was doing other markets; Petticoat Lane and Wembley on Sundays, and finding demand just as vigorous. By the end of the month she had vacated our flat and moved into her own one a few streets away.

I realised by now that I was in love with her. If, that is, the aching in the pit of my stomach and the thumping in my chest every time I was near her, was love. I told her as much when I got her alone in the flat, which was still reeking of the new Wilton carpets that had just been fitted.

'Am I supposed to be flattered?', she laughed.

'You could tell me whether or not you loved me', I replied angrily.

'I don't think I know what love is. And neither do you'. She pulled me close and we danced barefoot on the carpet. 'Isn't it enough that we like each other?'

'I love you', I insisted.

'Is that the kind of love that has marriage in mind?'

'The two generally go hand in hand, don't they?'

She pushed me away. 'You're not the marrying kind, Terry'.

'What's the marrying kind?'

'The kind that gets and keeps a regular job. The kind that takes out a mortgage, cuts the grass every week, gives his wife his wage packet on a Friday night. Is that the kind you are?'

'It doesn't have to be like that'.

'No? Tell me, then.'

'There's more than one way of skinning a cat'.

She laughed. 'Sure. Your gambling and thieving with Larry. And how long is that going to last? Before you get locked up, I mean?' She shook her head. 'You're the last person I'd marry, Terry - even if I did love you'.

Bitch. I wanted to slap her face. 'You're a fine one to talk'.

'Which is why I'm on the straight and narrow now. I don't ever want to see the inside of a prison. And you will, if you carry on the way you're going. Even Chris has seen the light'.

This was true. Flush with money from his High Street adventure, he had taken out a lease on a shop in Willesden Lane, and was selling second-hand furniture. He had bought a furniture van and done deals with several local auctioneers and estate agents to 'clear' houses and flats of furniture and effects when they came up for sale.

'There's no future in what you're doing', Tessa continued, 'not for you and me anyway'. She paused. 'If it's a partnership you're after, why not come in with me with the jewelery? It's going to get big, I know it, and I'm going to need a partner'

I hesitated. 'How would it work?'

'Simple. We pay ourselves a wage. What's left over goes into the bank and we use it to expand later on'.

'I've never had a bank account in my life'.

'I've got one; we can use that for a start...' She then launched into a long explanation of how it would work. Our responsibilities...the need for commitment...the rewards...

And so we became partners. To celebrate, we shared a bottle of cheap Australian wine then made love in front of the gas fire to the strains of Patsy Cline singing 'Three Cigarettes In An Ashtray'.

-

It wasn't long after this that I was to renew my acquaintance with Bannaher. A chance encounter with Fr Maguire was the catalyst. Hung-over from the previous night's excesses, I inexplicably found myself in a bed in a room in a ramshackle house on the edge of Wormwood Scrubs. There were also two snoring females in it. I recalled a gaggle of nurses at a party somewhere in the vicinity, but the rest was oblivion. Extricating myself from between the juddering mammarys, I decided that a brisk stagger around the common might be just the thing to clear my head. After a few minutes, however, I concluded that it might not. Unfortunately, Scrubs Lane on a Sunday morning has a lot in common with the outback, so I was forced to walk the mile or so back to civilisation. Nearing the Harrow Road (and the end of my tether), I concluded that the nearby church was as good a place as any to rest my feet. And a few prayers would hardly go amiss...

''Terence', beamed Fr Maguire, from the top of the steps, 'late as usual, I see...'

My life seemed criss-crossed with paths that always had Fr Maguire standing in the middle. Like the time I was an altar boy and hit him over the head with the collection box. I had been under the impression that another altar boy was coming into the sacristy and had hid behind the door, intent on scaring him. My surprise when the priest appeared instead resulted in him having a lump the size of a duck-egg on his bonce and to me losing my prestigious office. I wouldn't have minded so much, but at every wedding and funeral we took part in several crisp pound notes would be pressed into our sweaty little palms. Hopper McGrath, who had set me up, had to contend with painful goolies for a few days afterwards.

I had many run-ins with him after that; letters that went missing during the spell I had as temporary postman, his greyhounds escaping from their kennels, and, of course, the attempted burning of the school.

Standing on the steps of the little church in Scrubs Lane now, he looked anything but priestly. There was a strong smell of whiskey off him, and a look that suggested a night on the tiles. I knew the feeling.

'Rough night, Fr?' I asked.

He laughed. 'Well, it was lively, anyhow. I'm over for the annual county re-union. I'm surprised you missed it'.

I wasn't. All the ould fellas and ould wans talking about how good the old country was. If it was that good, why the fuck were they all over here, then?'

He told me how many people had died in the parish in the last year. That seemed to be the main topic of conversation over there. That and the weather. The first thing people scanned in the paper was the deaths column - to see if there was a funeral they could go to that day. It passed the time I suppose. He also told me that Rasher Rielly had found a vocation and was joining the priesthood. The little shit. I had caught him wanking once into the porridge vats at Drohans Mills - where I was a bag-humper and he was trainee progress chaser - and had got the sack for spreading malicious rumours about him. Idly, I wondered where one found a vocation; perhaps it was in the chest of drawers in his bedroom, under his prayer book but on top of the dirty pictures. Or maybe it was in his arse pocket all the time!

'Been to the White City yet Fr?' I asked, just to liven up the conversation. He looked blankly at me. 'The greyhound racing Fr?'

He smiled benignly, not biting.

'Temptation, Terence. Temptation. God works in mysterious ways, testing us, trying us. The path of righteousness is never an easy one, even for a priest'.

The ould hypocrite. It was rumoured that the Bishop had to bail him out when an irate bookie threatened to go to the papers about his debts.

'And what state is your immortal soul in, Terence?' he continued. 'Have you been practising your faith?

I had done more practising on my guitar in the last year - the one I no longer had - but that wasn't what he wanted to hear. He seemed satisfied when I told him I went to Mass most Sundays.

'Never lose the faith, Terence. Too many people who leave our shores cast themselves adrift in this city of sin. They become lost souls wandering aimlessly out of sight of the lord, worshipping false Gods, subjecting themselves to all the temptations of the flesh…' For a moment he got carried away. His voice had risen and some of the church-goers were giving him funny looks. He quickly changed the subject.

'Do you know where I'm off to now? To try and talk some sense into an eejit who has been living in a coffin in the backyard of a pub in Kilburn. I believe you know him...Mick Duggan?'

'Dougie?'

''The very man'.

I had read something about it in the Willesden Chronicle, but hadn't realised it was Dougie. From what I could gather, he was planning to spend a month underground for charity in the back garden at Mulligans.

'It takes a lot of guts', I said. 'And, sure, it's for a good cause'

'Is that what I'll tell his mother? That it's for a good cause? If he wanted to raise money for charity why didn't he do something normal? Like swimming the Channel or running from John O'Groats to Lands End?' He was getting quite agitated and I guessed he was under orders to get Dougie out of the coffin.

When I suggested I come with him he didn't object.

'I might be able to talk some sense into him'.

I didn't expect he would take a blind bit of notice, but it seemed as good a way as any of putting the Sunday morning down.

Gaining entrance to Mulligan's proved no problem. A couple of sharp raps on the side door and we were in. It was officially listed as a hotel, though inside there was little evidence of this. Its hole-in-the-wall appearance summed it up perfectly.

Even at this early hour there was a sprinkling of dour-faced drinkers at the bar. Hard-jaws by the look of them. A few eyebrows were raised as well as caps as the priest brushed by. We passed straight through the bar and headed for a passage that led to the back garden. Two high stools stood either side of the door with plastic buckets resting on them. Someone had stenciled a lopsided CHARITY LIE-IN on the wall behind. Some lie-in I thought and threw in two shillings.

I could hear muffled singing coming from somewhere in the garden. Looking around, I discovered it emanated from a plastic pipe. This pipe was about six inches in diameter, and was sticking up a similar distance above the ground. Judging by the quality of the singing, it was a fair bet that Dougie was already half-cut.

'Hello there, Dougie', I shouted down the pipe. 'Is that you?'

'Who the hell do you think it is...Lazarus?' replied a disembodied voice. 'Who's that?'

'Terry. Terry Byrnes'.

'I'd ask you to join me but there's not much room'. His laughter echoed up the pipe.

'How long do you plan to spend down there?

'Another few weeks…unless I get to like it'. The laughter continued.

'Is the pipe your only means of communication?'

'The only way, boy. Everything comes down and goes back up the same way'.

' Everything?'.

'The whole works, boy'.

I told him he was mad. Then I mentioned the charity bit.

This brought fresh laughter. 'Charity me hole! I'm not doing it for charity. I'm getting five hundred quid from Bannaher for it'.

'The subby?'

'The very man. He bought this kip a few weeks ago. The charity idea is a gimmick to get some publicity…'

This was too much for the priest, who had been hopping around like a hen on a hot griddle during our exchange. Pushing me out of the way, he bellowed down the pipe.

'I knew you weren't doing this out of the goodness of your heart, Duggan. Come up out of there at wance, before you have your mother in an early grave. What you're doing is a sin, a very grave sin. It's blasphemy…'

At that moment, Bannaher himself appeared. He was wearing a navy-blue suit, a button-down cream shirt open at the neck and a pair of patent-leather black shoes that you could almost use as toothpicks. I had a healthy dislike of people who managed to look so smooth that early in the morning.

He hadn't quite managed to steer the priest away from the pipe before the singing started again.

> 'Some say the devil is dead, the devil is dead, the devil is dead
> Some say the devil is dead, and buried in Killarney
> More say he rose again, rose again, rose again
> More say he rose again, and joined the British Army.

Fr. Maguire turned several shades of purple.

'He's drunk! My God, the man is fluthered!'

'Ah no. You see…' Bannaher almost physically dragged him away… 'It's the air down there, Fr, it gets a bit bad at times. Makes him ramble a bit. We pump fresh oxygen down every so often and that clears his head'

The priest sniffed. 'He sounded drunk to me. And then there's the question of personal gain. I heard a large sum being mentioned...'

'Ah no, Fr. He works for me you see, and it's true I am paying his wages while he is down there, but that's only fair, isn't it?' He paused 'We're always told that charity begins at home, aren't we? Now, when I was home on holiday the nuns at St Camilla's asked me if I could help out. And when I saw the state of the altar...well I...'

'I see. Very commendable'.

'If your own church had anything that needed doing...'

'Well, there is the sacristy roof...'

'No sooner said than mended. Come into my office and we'll work out the details...'

Two minutes later he was back. This time on his own. Just as Dougie was breaking into song again.

'Tell that eejit to shut his row...or I'll shut it for him'.

As I left, I wondered if Dougie's five hundred would ever materialise. I sincerely hoped he'd had the sense to ask for cash in advance.

## Chapter six

The acquisition of her own business had done something to Tessa, changed her. She had always been money-driven, but to see the naked ambition mirrored in her eyes every day now was disconcerting, even a little frightening. There was a missionary zeal about her; the mark of the converted was on her face; every day she was consumed by the desire to expand. No longer content to farm the markets every weekend, we had invested in a small Morris van and spent a considerable amount of time driving around the Capital, seeking new outlets. Tessa was convinced she had found the right one in a new shopping centre that had just opened out Hendon way. Here, several kiosks had been incorporated into the shopping mall, and one was still vacant. I didn't really have much say in the matter, and several weeks later, when we signed a one-year lease, our bank balance was greatly depleted by legal and other fees.

Tessa's midas touch hadn't deserted her; within a few weeks our turnover had exceeded all our expectations.

'Here's to the future, Terry', she said to me one evening. 'Kiosks in every shopping centre in the country, that's my ambition'.

I still wasn't convinced. Although we were making a good living, it was beginning to feel too much like hard work. We now had a girl employed running the kiosk, and I was spending most of my time driving around keeping our other outlets stocked up. More outlets only meant more work.

Being so busy meant that my relationship with Larry wasn't as close as it used to be. He still spent most of his afternoons in the betting shop, although some of his mornings were now taken up helping Chris in the shop.

Any free time I had I spent with Larry in the betting shops or going to the dogs. We went mostly to the evening meeting at Hendon or White City, though the afternoon meeting at Park Royal was a favourite haunt whenever we were free.

Larry, by now, was hooked on systems. He purchased them, he modified them, he invented them. But if he was making any money from them, I couldn't see it.

Park Royal was the place that changed all that. A weird sort of place on the fringes of the Western Avenue, cut off from both Acton and Ealing, it was surrounded by the railway marshalling yards of Willesden Junction and Harlesden. The North Circular Road, snaking around its outskirts, completed its encirclement.

It was a dreary landscape that I grew to know well. Tall chimneys jostling for prominence on the pylon-ravaged horizon, belching all kinds of shit into the atmosphere; galvanizers, zinc-platers, lead-smelters, other obnoxious plants all polluting without discrimination. The milkmen did well though; stomach-lining it was called. And the bosses were happy to pay; it was a damn sight cheaper than decent working conditions.

It was hard to imagine people living in the midst of al this but they did. Isolated pockets of grimy Victorian terraced houses poked their heads up along the narrow streets, like they had been spawned by their much bigger neighbours - although it was a fair bet that they were there long before the industrial estate.

Stranger still was the sight of the Central Middlesex Hospital sitting bang in the middle. This sprawling complex languished amidst the soot and grime, shit and slime, collectively inhaling whatever was floating about at any given time.

On reflection, perhaps it was the perfect set-up. The houses, the factories, the hospital, schools, pubs; there was even a crematorium somewhere in the vicinity - everything a body needed from the cradle to the grave.

Park Royal greyhound track was only a stone's throw from the hospital, not that we generally took too much notice of it as we hurried past to get to the track in time for the first race of the afternoon. Betting shops in those days were dreary places; there were no monitors, no TV''s, nothing only chalked-up prices and The Blower. Much better to go to the track and lose your money in style!

The Blower relayed the race commentaries to the shops - although not instantaneously as I accidentally discovered one afternoon. I was rushing for the first race, still several hundred yards from the track, when I heard the tell-tale shout from the track and knew the race was already underway. Cursing, I dived into the nearby betting shop, hoping to hear the tail-end of the race commentary, praying fervently that trap six wouldn't win. Imagine my surprise when the commentary didn't begin until almost half a minute later.

The significance of my discovery didn't sink in until later, when I met up with Larry at the track, and we were watching a race in progress.

'You know', he remarked as we watched a race in progress. 'This is a front-runners track. How many dogs leading at the halfway stage ever get beaten…?'

'Not many', I agreed. It was then that the significance of my knowledge hit me. A dog could run a long way in thirty seconds. Most races were half over at this point. When I voiced my opinions, he saw the implications straight away.

'Christ! Pity there's not a betting shop outside the track'.

It was a pity. The one I had just been in was less than three hundred yards from the track. But too far away all the same…

The thinking caps were on in earnest now.

The answer, of course, was walkie-talkies. All it needed was for one of us to be positioned in a suitable location to relay the trap number of any dog in a clear lead at half way. The receiver would be waiting around the corner from the bookies for the magic number; it would take only a couple of seconds to dash in and place the bet. All we had to do then was wait for the money to start rolling in!

Getting hold of the walkie-talkies wasn't too difficult, but they cost nearly a hundred pounds. They were just what we needed though - with a range of over a quarter of a mile. We carried out several trial runs to make sure we were within range of each other, then realised we needed to find a quiet spot from which to observe the races. It wouldn't do to be seen at the track speaking into a walkie-talkie!

The answer was staring us in the face: The Central Middlesex Hospital. Some of its buildings overlooked the track; there was bound to be a suitable vantage point somewhere. More importantly, we found that visitors could roam the grounds freely. This allowed us to select a flat-roofed building that gave us a clear view of the race. It was ideal in another sense too; it had an air-conditioning unit on the roof which provide ample screening from prying eyes.

Our plan was to rotate the operation in case the bookie got suspicious at seeing the same face collecting winnings all the time.

It pissed down that first afternoon. As the saying goes; 'You wouldn't put a dog out in it'. Indeed, they weren't out in it; they were snug in their kennels because racing had been put back half an hour. Only two idiots were soaking it up; one on the almost-obscured roof of a hospital building, the other skulking behind a betting shop in Acton Lane.

The rain eventually ceased and the racing got under way. I was on duty behind the betting shop that day, and every time Larry gave me a number I rushed into the shop and had a tenner on it. We were aware that not every race would suit our purposes; however, that first day provided four races, of which three produced winners, the fourth selection running wide at the last bend when still in front. We didn't care too much though; three winners at six to one, four to one, and two to one had given us a profit of more than a hundred pounds on the day.

Larry was hopping around the kitchen after the share-out.

'This is it Terry...the big one. We'll go to town now, boy!'

I had to admit to a sense of satisfaction myself. It had been my idea - not Larry's - and it was a success! We only had to operate it a few times a week and we would soon be rolling in it.

In a few months we had accumulated a lot of money. I had never seen so much, and neither had Larry. Chris and Tessa were agog. They couldn't believe it was so easy to manipulate the system.

'So simple', said Chris. 'And when you explain it, so obvious. I'm surprised no one else has thought of it'.

That was the beauty of it - Its simplicity. The one flaw in the bookmakers armour - that weak link that we searched so earnestly for - turned out to be nothing more than a handful of lost seconds on the one thing they prided themselves most on - their communications network.

'It didn't surprise me that no one else thought of it', said Larry, clapping me on the back. 'Only a really devious mind would make the connection'.

Chris said the possibilities were endless. We could extend it to other tracks and make a fortune.

'No', I said, 'We can only do it during the day, when betting shops are open. And only the tracks covered by The Blower'.

Hackney was the only other track used in the London area. There was an occasional service from Manchester White City or Perry Barr in Birmingham, but we didn't fancy all that travelling to the frozen North. As it turned out, Hackney wasn't suitable anyway. There wasn't a bookie's shop near enough to be within range of our walkie-talkies and the track.

Tessa, initially enthusiastic, was soon moaning.

'It won't last, Terry. Somebody will rumble it and you'll be caught. And where will that leave the business?'

By now we had opened another kiosk, this time in a new shopping arcade in Kilburn. Hiring another girl to run it, and taking on someone to help out in the van, meant we had joined the capitalist brigade almost overnight. This, to my way of thinking, put us in the same class as Bannaher and all the other exploiters - something I would never have thought possible a few months ago. It was, admittedly, Tessa's department - or so I told myself. She did all the hiring and firing, but I knew she wasn't exactly lavish with what she paid in wages because she couldn't help crowing about it.

'The business is doing fine', I replied. 'Sometimes I think it doesn't need me at all'.

'If you keep palming all the work off on Jeff, it won't', she retorted.

'So that's the way it is! Have you been spying on me? Or has that little shit been blabbing?'

'It is true then?' She gave me one of her sweetest smiles.

I didn't answer, but left, slamming the door behind me. By the time I got to the pub I had calmed down, by the time I had downed a brandy I was actually smiling. The scheming bitch didn't miss a trick!

She was right of course. Jeff was actually doing a lot of the work on his own while I loafed around in the betting shops or went to the dogs with Larry. I didn't really have the stomach for it anymore; it was just another job now. Besides, with the way the money kept rolling in I could afford to take it easy.

Tessa didn't see it that way. When I returned from the pub she started again.

'Look - are we going to make a go of it or not? I'm serious about it - even if you still treat it as a game'.

'Maybe that's the trouble. It was never my business in the first place'.

'What's that supposed to mean?'

I shrugged. 'It's your baby. Your ideas'.

'And you want out?'

I shrugged again.

'You're crazy! We haven't even begun. When it takes off - and it will - what you're making on your…your little racket will seem like small change'.

She had been shouting but now she quietened down. That was the way with her; suddenly the fire was gone from her eyes, to be replaced by something altogether more sensuous… all designed to persuade you that she desired you more than anyone else in the world. As usual I succumbed.

Later, as we lay intertwined on the settee, she broached the subject again,

'Do you know what we were offered today?'

'What?' I asked, drowsily.

'A group of kiosks - three - all under cover in the Camden Market area. All selling magazines at present, but the agent told me that a change of use would be no problem'.

''Forget it', I told her, felling her nipples grow hard again under my fingers. 'We can't afford it'.

'There is one way'. She nibbled at my ear as she whispered into it. 'With the money you and Larry are making we could easily swing it. We could make him a partner'.

I was awake now. 'Larry? I don't think he'd go for it. You know how he feels about work'.

'He could be a silent partner'. She spoke airily. 'I've already spoken to him and I think he's in favour'.

Is he now? I said to myself, sitting up and lighting a Kensitas. Good old Larry, what did he think I was - a fucking mushroom? Keeping me in the dark and feeding me bullshit. I had spoken to him less than an hour ago and not a word had crossed his lips.

'It's dirty money, Tessa. I thought you were on the straight and narrow these days?'

She laughed. 'If it gets me what I want I don't care where it comes from. Besides, there's nothing dishonest in using it, is there?'

She was right again of course. The money was clean now. I suddenly saw with a clarity that I had never experienced before that she was using me. And had been all along. She was loving and affectionate to be sure, but it was all part of her scheme to make it to the top. And now she had entangled Larry in her web. What had she promised - indeed already delivered - to him?

The only weapon I had was the money. As long as I held onto it I still exercised some control. Money was power, and I wasn't about to relinquish it - not yet.

'Give me a few days to think it over', I said as I stubbed out the cigarette.

'What's there to think about?' Her hand snaked sensuously over my groin. It's the opportunity of a lifetime - don't blow it'.

-

Our social life became hectic. Well, we were the new rich. We could afford to live it up. Unfortunately, we were still prisoners of our own class - or lack of it. We could have been having a rare ould time in the West End night-spots; instead we were still frequenting the grotty Irish pubs and clubs of NW London.

After a night at the Gresham or Galtymore dance halls we would turn up at Mulligans. Well, we still called it Mulligans, though the sign over the door now read The Hooley (prop P Bannaher) It didn't matter if it was the middle of the night, The Hooley was open all hours. There was a well-aired joke that the cops revved up as they passed by. Guilty consciences I suppose.

There was no doubt that it had acquired a certain notoriety since our subby friend purchased it. The charity lie-in had the desired effect; the tabloids lapping up the story. Bannaher got his picture splashed across most of the dailies - his ugly countenance smirking out at me from every corner shop and news-stand.

49

He wasn't one to let fame slip quietly by him and he milked the story for all it was worth. The media played their part and there were several human-interest stories; one of them had portrayed Dougie as a dare-devil ex-army demolitions expert who had at one time fought against the Balubas in the Congo - and had almost been et for his troubles. It was the first time I had heard he's been in the army, never mind the Congo!

There was, however, one thing the papers didn't have; a picture of this mighty warrior. And Bannaher made sure it stayed that way. The only photos would be those of Dougie emerging from the coffin when it was all over. And Bannaher casually informed them that unless they made him a reasonable offer he was quite prepared to have him emerging wearing a bag over his head.

'It is for charity, after all!'

In the end, he negotiated an exclusive deal with one of them. Pictures, story, the lot. It was rumoured he got thousands. No one knew for sure, but whatever the figure, Dougie saw little of it. His immediate take, when he did finally emerge, was two hundred quid, shoved inside his pocket by a beaming Bannaher as he hugged him for the 'exclusive'.

Asked what his first requests were, Dougie replied; 'A pint and a shave'. He was treated to the first, but the shave had to wait until after his triumphal procession down Kilburn High Road on the back of a tipper lorry - owned - naturally, by Bannaher.

That was about as good as it got for Dougie. The rest of his promised five hundred never materialised. Instead, Bannaher told him he could have free pints for six months. It was a master stroke. The punters rolled up in their droves to have a look at him, and all of them wanting to buy him a pint!

Once Bannaher got the punters inside he planned to keep them there. Long enough to lighten their pockets anyhow. Internally, the place was a cross between a whore-house and a rent-a-navvy agency. The subbies were there dispensing subs to the needy, but only to those judged capable of wielding a pick-and-shovel in a few hours time. And the misfortunate recipients were falling over each other trying to ingratiate themselves with their erstwhile employers.

The whores were there too; painted Irish versions, who, for a few pounds, would whisk you upstairs to taste the delights of their not-so-fresh-anymore flesh. And have someone else ransack your clothes if you were foolish enough to hang them in the place suggested.

Tessa towed along with us one night to see Bannaher's latest gimmick; a mock-up coffin on stage, with Dougie rising from it on the stroke of midnight. Count Dracula of Kilburn! How he got Dougie to agree to be part of such a circus was beyond me, but then, Dougie had never seemed quite the same man since his 'resurrection'.

I could see by the expression on Tessa's face that she had never seen anything remotely like this before.

'What is <u>that</u> smell?', she asked, wrinkling her nose.

'Crubeens', replied Larry. 'Haven't you ever heard of crubeens?' She looked blankly at him.

'Pigs trotters. They're a delicacy in Ireland'.

They were never a delicacy in our house. Any more than pigs heads were. They were all we could afford at times. I could still see the occasional pig's head sitting on the big willow plate in middle of the kitchen table. Well, half a pig's head actually. Me staring at it, and it staring back at me with its one eye, its one ear and its half a nose. Then we would devour it with rare savagery; Fergus and myself fighting over who got the ear or the tongue.

Tessa stared in disbelief as someone bought a couple of crubeens from the pot bubbling away behind the counter. He wrapped them in a newspaper, then shoved them in his pocket, still dripping.

'That'll do nicely for the breakfasht', he said, winking at her.

She gave him a look that would puncture a lung. I could see why. Badly dressed didn't describe him; badly undressed was nearer the mark. The seat of his trousers was down behind his knees, and the top of his arse was glinting at us through the smoke-haze as he retreated.

I watched him lumber away, a pint in one hand and a crubeen in the other, and was reminded again about the relationship between men and bogs.

In a few hours time he would down some hole - probably working for Bannaher - covered in shite. And this time tomorrow night he would be here again, looking and behaving exactly the same. What sort of life was that? Far better if he stayed down his fucking hole and had someone fill it in on top of him!

'You can see the skid marks on his arse', Larry shook his head. 'Thick as shit - and happy with it'.

'I cannot understand how people can live like that', said Tessa.

I understood only too well. They were innocents abroad. It wasn't their fault if the were uneducated or unskilled. They were the Jonjo's of this world;

ignorant of the ways of the big city. The fault lay with the country that forced them to live in a foreign land. London might just as well be Mars to them so different was it from the hill farms and boglands of the Western Seaboard that nurtured them. There but for the grace of God went I!

Like a spider, Bannaher wove his web. Luring the punters inside then executing his strategy to keep them there. Music was supplied by the resident band - an accordion and guitar duo who sang American country-and western songs in Kerry accents. There was a set of drums also, that sat silent until Bannaher himself deigned to play them. Then he banged away and sang rebel songs in a raucous, compelling voice.

He cut the cost of changing cheques to two and a half percent. He claimed he was paring costs to the bone.

'What fucking costs' snarled Larry. 'Aren't most of the cheques his own'.

Sometimes one of the whore did a striptease on stage to liven the night up. Afterwards, you could see a steady stream of customers heading upstairs.

On weekends Dougie held centre stage. Like Jesus, he arose and appeared to many. On the stroke of midnight. If he managed to stay sober that is. Sometimes he climbed in early and fell asleep.

Tonight he'd had an early one. Bannaher rolled the drums; the lights dimmed; canned smoke swirled around the coffin. No Dougie. Bannaher eventually lifted the lid and poked inside with his drumstick.

'Come on you drunken bum, wake up'. Dougie, however, had overdone it - and could be heard being sick inside. This was too much for the subby; he slammed the lid shut and told the band to play a tune.

Things started to go downhill from then. Someone started an argument with one of the barmen because he wouldn't change his cheque. Bannaher finished the argument by head-butting him and stretchering him on the floor. He then dragged him by the legs towards the door shouting; 'tell Donoghue his cheques are no good here'. He threw the offending cheque out the door; 'there it goes, bouncing all the way back to Cricklewood'.

Dougie, meanwhile, had made a belated appearance, moaning and sighing with great verve, his white robe billowing behind him. His attempt at a dramatic appearance was doomed however; nobody seemed to be taking a blind bit of notice of him.

All except Bannaher, that is. ''Shut your fucking row', he roared , the business at hand taken care of, 'and get back in your box'. He then calmly struck up a tune with the band, and soon the place was filled with the strains of Danny Boy, as if nothing had happened.

About an hour later Donoghue turned up, flanked by members of The Sunshine Gang. They carried lumps of lead piping and bicycle chains. Several of them swung their chains like hammer throwers, scattering the crowd to the farmost corners, while Donoghue picked up a glass and headed for Bannaher. Donoghue was a red-faced younger version of Bannaher himself, reputedly even worse to work for.

'This is the rock you perish on, you Mayo cunt', he shouted, hurling himself at the subby. Bannaher, who had been flicking dirt off his jacket-sleeve, raised his hands instinctively, a look of fear in his eyes. I was close-by and managed to divert the lunging fist. It smashed into the bar support behind his head, the pint glass clenched in it smashing into smithereens.

The barmen, meanwhile, hadn't been idle, dispensing baseball bats from a stockpile behind the counter. By now tables and chairs were sailing through the doors as well as customers. I lost contact with Tessa and Larry, and when I tried to get out I found myself trapped between the swinging chains and the swiping bats. It was inevitable that something would connect. I felt a searing pain in my arm as I raised it to protect my head, then a burning sensation in my chest as I staggered across the room. The last thing I saw was Bannaher with his arm around someone's head, banging it against the counter then I blacked out.

# Chapter seven

The doctor held the x-ray before him and studied it for a moment. Seemingly satisfied, he attached it to the clipboard then wrote something on my file.

'Well Mr Byrne', he smiled at me,' how are we this morning?'

'We' felt fine. 'We' wanted to get out of this shaggin' hospital.

'Never better, doctor. When can I get out?'

He shook his head. Not for another while I'm afraid'. He wagged his finger. 'You're lucky to be alive, young man'.

When he was gone, Nurse Mahony plumped my pillows and straightened the bedclothes.

'He's right, you know. Another half inch and it could have been curtains for you. You have a tear in your lung that size'. She held up a thumb and forefinger to indicate. 'Just be thankful you're still with us'.

'I am, Jock, I am'.

'And stop calling me Jock. My name is Mary'.

'You're not a relation of Jock Mahony - that star of countless bad westerns?' I put on my best western drawl. 'With a handle like that, ma'm, I wuz shore you wuz related'.

'How long more will I have to stay?' I asked when she had finished snickering.

She considered for a moment. 'Two weeks, maybe. Even then you'll have to take it easy for ages after'. She laughed. 'You can forget about work for a while'.

*I'd forgotten about work long ago*, I was tempted to say. Still, I didn't want to disillusion Mary; a plump, cheery-faced girl from Sneem, who somehow had the impression that I was hard-working and industrious. She wasn't the worst of them; that honour went to the ward Sister, a hatchet-faced ould bitch that was starched inside as well as out.

'Mary'. I said, 'I want to whisper something to you'.

'What?' She was leaning over me, and her tits were threatening to burst through her uniform.

'Is it true that you nurses do be naked under them uniforms?'

'Get away with you. Terry', she said, blushing back to her ears. 'Who told you that?

'Is it true, though?', I persisted.

'That's for you to find out', she said breathlessly, patting the already-plumped pillows. Out of the corner of my eye I saw the Sister striding purposefully down the corridor. Mary saw her too and moved away, but not before whispering; 'I'm on nights next week'.

By now I had been here three weeks, and every day had been a drag. Not that I remembered much of the first week; I had been so drugged up with morphine and other drugs that the days had passed in a blur. I knew I'd had visitors, but who they were and what we had spoken about I couldn't recall.

Later on, sometime during the second week, Tessa told me I had looked like a zombie for so long they had been worried I would never return to my old self. She helped me to piece together what had happened. Apparently, one of the barmen had mistook me for a member of The Sunshine Gang, and had fractured my arm with a blow from his baseball bat. I had the stumbled against one of the gang, who, in turn, mistook me for one of the barmen, and he had, apparently, stuck a knife in me. When the fight ended I was found lying under a table, unconscious.

During that second week the cops paid me a visit. I got the impression they were more interested in the participants in the fight than in my injuries, so I pretended I knew nobody and asked if anyone had been 'done' for the attack on me. I got a gruff reply that enquiries were still going on.

Larry told me later what was bugging the cops; *nobody was saying anything*. Whatever limbs and heads had been busted, they had all been spirited away before the police arrived. Larry said Bannaher was planning to mete out his own punishment for the damage that had been done. Knowing him, I didn't doubt it.

'I got a punctured lung because of that bastard', I said. 'He could at least have sent a box of chocolates'.

'That'll be the day. He reckoned it was your own fault for getting in the way'.

'I saved his ugly mug from looking even uglier!' I explained that Donoghue had tried to re-arrange his features, and but for my intervention would probably have succeeded. 'That must count for something when the free drinks are being distributed'.

'I wouldn't count on it'.

I laughed. 'No, neither would I'. I was just thankful I was still in one piece. Retribution could wait; of more concern right now was the ongoing success of the Park Royal operation.

'Not to worry', Larry said, 'it's all in hand. Chris is standing in till you get back on your feet'.

Tessa hadn't said anything more about the money, so I collared him about it now.

'I understand you don't mind giving our money to Tessa',

'What do you mean? Aren't we all in it together?' He looked at me. 'Well, aren't we?'

'I suppose so'. I spoke wearily. 'You're in favour then?'

'It seems sound to me. I spoke to Chris - he's fairly shrewd on these matters - and he said we'd be mad not to'.

These were almost identical to Tessa's words to me. I had never been sure of her relationship with Chris; now I began to wonder if it was something deeper than mere friendship.

'Won't it go against your principles, having to work for a living?' I couldn't keep the sarcasm from my voice.

If he noticed, it didn't show. 'There'll be no reneging on them. The only part of me that'll be working is my money'. He must have sensed my misgivings. 'You don't have any objections to becoming rich, I take it?'

I hadn't. I just wasn't convinced that throwing everything we had at Tessa was the best way to achieve it.

During my fourth - and hopefully my last - week in hospital, I began to get the feeling that something was wrong. What it was I couldn't put my finger on, but the feeling persisted. By now I was up and around most of the day, prowling the corridors, feeling like a tiger in a cage. I still wasn't allowed outside, so I often passed the time in the lounge area trying to identify the chimney stacks visible through the windows. The foundry...the lead smelter...the bakery...the galvanizers...Christ, there were so many.

The dog track was on the other side of the hospital, so wasn't visible. But sometimes to my delight I could hear the faint roar of the crowd in the distance as the dogs left the traps. Wednesday afternoon, all through the race times, I strained my ears for a sound. Nothing. Not a dickey-bird. Perhaps the wind was in the wrong direction. Ah well...Larry and Chris were out there somewhere, making money for us.

Later still, driven by boredom, I flicked through a pile of newspapers and came across a headline; PARK ROYAL SOLD FOR DEVELOPMENT. LAST RACE TODAY. Stunned, I read it again. It was dated last Friday.

Confused, I stumbled back to the ward. Why hadn't I been told? What the fuck was going on?

In the evening, Chris turned up, and plonked a bunch of grapes on the bed.

I flung them aside. 'Why didn't you tell me?'

'Tell you what?'

I picked up the newspaper and held it up for him to see. 'This'.

He shrugged. 'I didn't know'.

I looked at him in disbelief. 'You must have! It was last Friday, remember? You were meeting Larry at the track after you left here…or so you said'.

'But I didn't. Not until I got to the track. None of us did'. He tried to conjure up a smile. 'Let's be honest, Terry, none of us are great newspaper readers'.

That much was true. Magazines yes; but Titbits or Penthouse didn't cover a lot of dog-racing. Still, I found it hard to believe that Larry hadn't come across the news somewhere in his racing paper.

'That's it then', I said, feeling deflated. 'We'll never find such easy pickings again'.

'There must be somewhere else'.

'There's nowhere fucking else. That's it. Kaput'. Now that I had calmed down, I could see that Chris was on edge. 'Come on. Something's bothering you.' A thought occurred to me…'Where is everyone? You're the only one I've seen since Friday'.

'That's what I came to tell you about. They're in Scotland'.

'Where in Scotland?'

'No. Tessa and Larry have gone to Scotland'.

'That's what I thought you said. What are they doing in sweaty-sockland? 'I don't really know'.

'Don't know or won't say?' I grabbed his hand and held it against my forehead. 'First the dog track. Now you tell me half the gang have emigrated. Tell me I'm hallucinating'.

'You're not hallucinating. He paused, 'They'll tell you all about it when they get back'.

'Oh, they are coming back then? I spoke sarcastically. 'This year or next?' My attempt at a laugh fell flat. 'With Tessa you can never be sure'.

'This weekend as far as I know'. He spoke quietly.

'What business could they have in bonnie Scotland? We haven't opened up a shop there, have we?' I thought I detected an amused glint in his eyes. 'Ah Jaysus, don't tell me it's a dirty weekend? Sure they could have that at home - the coast being clear, as they say'.

'Look, it's none of my business what they're up to. Or yours for that matter'.

'You'd say that, would you? What if it concerned our business - mine and Tessa's - wouldn't that be my business?' I felt angry now. 'Just tell me, Chris, what the fuck is going on?'

'You're asking the wrong man, Terry'. He looked at his watch. 'I have to go. Don't do anything rash until the weekend'.

When he had gone I pondered on his last bit of advice. Why should I have to do anything the weekend? Maybe it was the way he phrased it. Lying back on my bed, I tried to piece together our conversation to see if I had missed something. I realised it wasn't so much what he had said as what he hadn't. Oh, he knew what was going on alright!

I fell asleep and dreamt I was being chased through Edinburgh by fierce-looking highland fighting men astride giant horses. The horses were as big as elephants; every highlander was kited out in a tartan kilt and jacket, and carried a huge shield attached to his left arm. The other hands held a variety of weapons, maces, spears, and large cannon-balls that they lobbed continuously at me. They finally cornered me against the battlements of the castle, where I deflected as best I could the missiles raining down on me, using a dustbin lid which I had somehow acquired.

Then the missiles ceased and I realised that all the faces were identical; bushy ginger beards covering everything except noses and eyes. Two of the riders moved forward a pace and peeled their 'faces' away, revealing themselves as Tessa and Larry.

'Why?' I shouted. 'Why Scotland?' Then something thumped me on the shoulder and I woke up to find Mary leaning over me.

'You were having a nightmare. Something about Scotland'. She must have come on duty while I was asleep. 'You alright?'

'Nothing that a good feel wouldn't cure', I whispered, letting my hand brush against her starched chest.

'Not here', she blushed. 'And not now'.

Mary was my salvation. The one pin-prick of light in an otherwise miserable black hole. All day long I had to suffer the false good-cheer of the ward Sister. Long walks and lungfuls of fresh air were her remedies for almost every ailment. I spent most of my time shutting the windows that she opened. When I told her that the air in a gas chamber was probably better than that around Park

Royal the atmosphere became even frostier. Her revenge was painful jabs of penicillin in my arse.

Mary's first night on the graveyard shift, as she called it, was a revelation. Sometime after midnight, when I was dozing off, she brought me a bedpan.

'I thought you might need this', she said, pulling the screen around the bed. Before I could protest, she held her fingers to her lips. Then she sat on the edge of the bed and shoved her hand under the blankets. I had been playing with myself, so it didn't require much effort on her part.

'Looks like I came along just in time'. She laughed as she wiped her hand.

'That's the best medicine I've had in weeks', I whispered. 'Does everyone get this treatment?'.

'Only those I like, Sure it helps to pass the long nights'.

It did too. Every night she came and administered her treatment. Sometimes she let me feel her tits or between her legs, but as her uniform couldn't appear disheveled, my fumbling was very basic.

' I know it's a sin, but, sure, you poor fellas in here need something to take your minds off your troubles'.

'You mean there's others!' I laughed. 'Oh, Mary, you're an awful woman'.

'I always make an act of contrition afterwards'. She nudged me. 'Anyway, I like the feel of mens' things in my hand. One minute they're pieces of liquorice, the next sticks of rock'.

Since she liked sweets so much I should have asked her if she would like to suck a gobstopper!

By the weekend I had other worries on my mind. No one had been to see me since Chris' visit and I was wondering what the fuck was going on. On Monday, Mary, who was back on days, remarked on it.

'Nice friends you have. They haven't been to see you for ages'.

I was desperate. 'Mary', I said, 'what would happen if I discharged myself? Something's going on and I need to find out what'.

'You can't do that!' She looked horrified.

'Why not? I feel fine'.

'In here you do. But you could undo all the good work of the doctors and everybody else if you discharged yourself. If you had a relapse the hospital wouldn't be pleased. I know I wouldn't't'.

'What am I going to do then? Up until a week ago I thought I had a business and three good friends. Now I don't know if I have anything'.

She shook her head. 'It's not right the way they treat you'. She seemed to be considering. 'I could try and find out something after I finish work if you like'.

I gave her the addresses and tried to lose myself in a book about a gang of criminals in Brighton. The young hero, if that's what he could be called, was named Pinky, and was a nasty piece of work. I wondered how The Sunshine Gang would fare if they came up against him and his cronies. Not very well, I reckoned.

Tuesday morning Mary was busy for a long time, and it was well into the day before she had time to come and speak to me.

'Nobody was at the second address'. This was Tessa's flat. 'I spoke to the woman downstairs and she said nobody had been around for weeks'. She paused and looked at me. 'Is Tessa your girlfriend?'

'Does it look like it?'

'The woman also said that she had seen Tessa and a man load up some suitcases in a white car one morning. She thinks that was the last time she saw them'.

Larry and the bitch heading for Scotland. Why all the secrecy though? I had long ago accepted that Tessa wasn't going to return my love, so I could hardly lay claim to much of a relationship with her. A convenient fuck, that's all we were to each other. Maybe not even that anymore.

'And Chris, did you see him?'

'Yes. He's busy apparently. Another shop. He said you'd understand'. She looked at me so I nodded. I understood alright - I was getting the run-around.

'He said he'll try and make it tomorrow'.

In the end, it wasn't Chris who turned up, but Bernie. And then not for several days. I hadn't seen her for some time because Chris hadn't been seeing much of her of late.

She placed a large bag of chocolates and fruit on the bedside locker and kissed me. There was a taste of brandy on her lips.

'I had no idea, Terry, she said, sitting down. She indicated the bag. 'We had a whip-round at work. The chocolates are liqueur - the strongest I could find'

I sampled a few of them straight away. Creamy cups brimming with a syrupy substance that tasted almost entirely of brandy.

'Thank the girls for me', I said between munches. 'I suppose you heard from Chris'.

She nodded. 'Only yesterday. I was home on holidays for a few weeks'. She made a face. 'Men are all bastards, aren't they?'

'Women too'. We both laughed.

'I can see how you would feel that way. After what Tessa did...', she stopped, sensing something was wrong.

'What? Come on, spit it out...'

'Well...' She was flustered. 'Her and Larry...getting married like that...' her voice trailed off,

I almost fell off the bed. I had visualised the pair of them doing many things, but getting married wasn't one of them.

'You didn't know?'

I shook my head.

'The bastard. The dirty, rotten bastard. Oh Chris, you bastard...' Tears appeared in her eyes and she wiped them angrily away. 'He used me to...to...what a rotten trick to play...' She stood up abruptly. 'I'm going round there...'

'Don't go, Bernie'. I placed a hand on her arm. 'Not yet...'

She sat down again. 'I'm sorry, Terry. But you see what he's done...'

I saw only too well. Got someone else to do the dirty work. I wondered where the lovebirds were. Still in Scotland, waiting for it to blow over, I guessed.

'What else did he say?'

'Not much. I think they went to Gretna Green'.

That's where couples elope to'.

''It's also the place to get married without too many formalities. A couple of days and not too many questions asked. Why were they in such a hurry? Was she pregnant?'

I doubted it. I was beginning to think she might not be human at all, but a devil. A she-devil in disguise. Christ, Larry, but you don't know what you're letting yourself in for!

Then I remembered the money. Our money. Larry's and mine. Larry had been accountant, banker and cashier all rolled into one. Keeping our money safe and secure under the floorboards in his bedroom. Was it still safe and secure there, I wondered?

# Chapter eight

It wasn't, of course. The gaping hole beneath the floorboards was proof of that. I sat down heavily on the bed and stared morosely at the floor. By now the shock had worn off, partly because I had been half expecting it, but it was still a wrench to see my fears confirmed.

I didn't think Larry had it in him. But then, he was only human. And when Tessa had decided to wrap those long legs around his scrawny frame and whisper endearments in his earlug, it was inevitable that he would succumb. I didn't condone it, but I could understand it.

It was three days now since Bernie had dropped her bombshell, and the intervening time in hospital had been wretched. Deep down I knew what to expect; I knew I had been turned over. But it still hurt.

Bernie had returned the following day having failed to get ant joy from Chris. His argument was that it wasn't his business - if Larry and Tessa didn't see fit to tell me themselves, then he wasn't their bloody messenger!

The only good news was the doctor's reluctant release of me from hospital. This came about only because I convinced him that I had a loving family environment to return to. I almost laughed; my best friend had stolen my girl and my business and done a runner with my money - now there was a loving environment!

That the money and the business had gone I had no doubt. The only agreement I had with Tessa was verbal. Everything else - the bank account, the leases, the kiosks - were in her name. I was willing to bet my life that the money from our cash-box was now in her account. Marrying Larry was only a means to an end. It had to be. The poor bastard didn't know what he was letting himself in for. Not that I felt any sympathy. 'I hope you die roaring, you cunt' I shouted at the empty room.

I sat there, hardly moving, as it grew dark around me. From the darkness I watched the trains scuttling past the back window, the images in the lighted carriages reminding me of the what-the-butler-saw machines we'd played in Brighton not so long ago.

It was near midnight when Chris returned. I heard his key in the lock, then the click as he flicked the light switch. He didn't see me for a moment, his attention drawn to the hole in the floor.

'How much would you say there was, Chris?'

He didn't even flinch to give him his due. Turning slowly to face me, he adopted a stance that made me think he was expecting me to rush him.

'Before you jump to conclusions, Terry, we had a break-in'.

I began to laugh. Jesus, did I laugh. I laughed so much the tears ran down my face.

'Oh Christ, that's a good one. The best yet. I supposed you called in the old bill'.

'Straight away, he replied, poker-faced. 'They came and took fingerprints and stuff, but they don't seem too optimistic'.

That was when I decided to hit him. A long, loping right aimed at the smirk. It was all over in a moment. I lay gasping with pain as my hand was twisted behind my back. I hadn't realised it, but I was as weak as a straw.

'People just out of hospital shouldn't throw punches', he said. 'It's bad for their constitution'. He twisted a bit harder. 'I haven't got time for this. I've told you what happened, you can believe it or not. And as for the wedding, it's a free country'. He released my hand suddenly.

I rubbed my arm. 'You're all bastards. Why? What did I do to deserve this?'

He didn't reply, but kicked the pieces of flooring towards the hole. 'I think you should move out'.

'What, tonight?'

'There's no rush. Tomorrow will do'. A pause. 'It might be… embarrassing, you know…when…' He didn't finish but turned on his heel. 'I've just remembered someone I've got to visit'.

When he had gone I packed everything of mine. There wasn't much. One suitcase. Then I started emptying wardrobes, piling the contents in a heap in the middle of the sitting room floor. Books newspapers, clothes, shoes, everything was included in the heap. The TV and stereo followed. The bigger furniture came next. Finally, I dragged the carpet over the heap. Then I sprinkled lighter fuel over the clothes and magazines and set fire to the lot. When it was burning nicely I picked up my case and left.

-

'Chris is on the warpath'. Bernie dropped her shopping on the kitchen table and looked at me. 'I think you should go on holiday somewhere'.

'He doesn't know I'm here, does he?'

'Not yet. But how long before he finds out? Especially with that…' She indicated towards the window…'out there'.

'That' was our van - mine and Tessa's - that I had taken from outside Jeff's digs the night I started the fire. That was almost a week ago, and I was feeling much stronger now, much more able to cope with the world. It was only money

I'd lost; the business I'd never really wanted anyhow. If it meant that much to the bitch she could have it - and good riddance. There were a few scores to settle, but they could wait.

Bernie knew most of what had happened, what I hadn't told her she had pieced together herself. Since I had moved in with them, she and her flatmate Annie had been very good to me. Indeed, their mothering instincts had only been looking for an excuse to surface, and the fussed over me like a pair of hens.

Bernie had been back to the flat and said it was a real mess - although the fire brigade had got there before too much damage was caused. Chris had moved out and was kipping in one of his shops.

'What did you see in him?' I asked her now.

'What did Lady Chatterley see in Mellors?'

'Who's she when she's about?'

'You've been sitting on her most of the week'. She picked up a book from the settee and threw it at me.

I looked at the title; Lady Chatterley's Lover. 'What is it, a love story?'

She laughed. 'You could say that, I suppose'.

'And where does Mellors fit in?'

'He's the gardener'.

'Chris, the gardener?' I shook my head. 'I don't think so. He wouldn't settle for such a lowly position. Not anymore'. I handed the book back and she tossed it back on the settee.

'It's such a stupid story anyway. Totally unbelievable. Almost as unbelievable as Larry and Tessa. What do you think she sees in him?'

'You **are** joking!'

'The money? But he was putting that in anyway. You said so yourself'.

'And now she's got mine too'. I saw her look at me and shrugged. 'I was … undecided'.

Annie came in at that moment and threw herself on the battered Chesterfield, saving me further explanations.

'Guess what? The lovebirds are back. And she's sporting a diamond…' she fluttered her hand…'as big as a mushroom'.

Bernie looked at me. I said nothing.

'And guess what else?' she continued with hardly a pause, 'when she was gone I spoke to Denise on the stall…' She looked at Bernie…'you know Denise, her that worked at Smiths a while back? - well anyway, she said they were expanding even more soon, and that she would be in charge of a whole area then'.

I stood up. It was time to move out. 'I guess you're right, Bernie. It's about time I looked up those old friends of mine across the river'.

There were no old friends, and I didn't cross the river. But I had to get away before I did something I regretted. It wasn't that I was afraid of a confrontation, but for the moment I had been out-maneuvered. A tactical withdrawal was how Pinky would have described it.

After a while, I found myself spending more and more time in the Euston area. I was drawn to the two magnificent railway Stations, Euston and Kings Cross, no more than a stone's throw from each other, and by the end of a week was parking there on a more or less permanent basis. I bought a mattress for the van, and began using the stations themselves for my personal hygiene. In the morning I would wash, shave and breakfast at one. This would be followed by a leisurely read of the racing paper, the afternoon taken care of in the betting shop. In the evenings I invariably got pissed.

However, getting legless every night soon loses its lustre, and a few weeks of it sobered me up. Ii was still hurting but I realised that the bottle wasn't the answer. I took to watching the passing parade; the swamping of the station during the rush hours, and the empty, lonely platforms late at night, and I realised there were others out there just as mixed up, just as forlorn as myself. They were runaways mostly, or dropouts. From their families, from hostels, sometimes from life itself. Their bed for the night was usually a bench in the station. Many of the girls were willing to swap that bench for a bed, even if that bed was only a mattress in the back of a van. Even if it meant sharing the mattress.

It didn't take me long to discover that living didn't come much cheaper out of the back of a van. Expenses still had to be found; food and drink still had to be consumed, the bookie had to be accommodated. I had a couple of hundred salted away - my emergency fund - but it was clear that I was going to be skint again fairly soon. Not that being broke was a new experience; but it wasn't a pleasant one, and was one that I didn't plan to repeat.

Since it was clear that all the schemes with Larry were now either or inoperable, I spent some time considering my options. I never once considered getting a job; no, there were easier ways of making a living. Then it hit me - scrap metal. Scrap metal merchants were paying good prices for lead copper and brass, and London was full of empty or derelict buildings. I became an expert at removing lead flashing quickly from the roofs of the empty factories that dotted the Park Royal area. A sharp Stanley knife was all that was needed to trim off the exposed flashing, roll it into a compact coil, then drop it to the ground below. Inside the building was a similar story; copper piping was easily cut through using a hacksaw, and brass doorknobs and other fittings were easily removed using a screwdriver.

Soon I never ventured anywhere without my three trusty tools; my Stanley knife, my hacksaw and my screwdriver. I became very conscientious; every morning, around seven, I sallied forth and mingled with the legitimate work traffic, carried out my day's work, and was breakfasting in The Ace by ten-o-clock.

I was unlikely to bump into any of my old friends there at that time of the day, I reasoned. Or at any time of the day I soon found out; they hadn't been there for a long time. Well, it was understandable…The Ace was beneath them now wasn't it? All right for the likes of me, a person of no fixed abode, part of the flotsam and jetsam, but they were above all that now. Hah!

Not beneath Dougie though. His excessive drinking had caused Bannaher to dump him - with the result he now had neither a job nor fame. His mornings were spent sobering up in the Ace, until they too got fed up and chucked him out. After that he took to sleeping in the graveyard up Neasden Lane, and shouting poetry at bewildered passers-by

Last night I had a dream
Beyond the Isle of Skye
I saw a dead man win a fight
And I think that man was I

One morning, towards the end of November, I was thawing out in the Ace, when Freda, the cook, handed me a letter. It had been left there for me by Bernie, whom I had not seen since the day I'd moved out.

It was from my mother.

'*Son*', she wrote, '*I hope this finds you. The telegram we sent was not delivered. Fergus is gone from us…a tragic accident. Your father won't forgive you for not being at the funeral…he won't even mention your name now…*'

Inside was a cutting from the local paper:

Local Man Gored To Death

Fergus O'Byrne died last night in a bizarre incident involving a car and a tractor. The car had tried to overtake the tractor but oncoming traffic forced it to take avoiding action, causing it to run into the back of the tractor. The passenger, identified as Fergus O'Byrne, was speared to death by the prong on the fork-lift attachment fixed to its rear.

The car driver, still clearly in shock, told our reporter on the scene; *'I pulled out to overtake the tractor, not realising there was a dip in the road. Suddenly a lorry appeared on the brow of the hill and I was forced to pull back. The tractor braked and I ran up its behind. There was a cock-lifter attached and the fork went through the headlight, right in front of where Fergus was sitting. I never saw it...it was getting dark...'*

A Garda spokesman said later that it was a tragic affair, a million-to-one chance, and warned about overtaking in poor light.

The cutting was dated almost a month previously.

I didn't cry. I couldn't. I escaped from the Ace and began driving. Anywhere. I don't think I even realised I was driving; my auto-pilot was making all the moves, I was just going along for the ride.

Fergus dead. My big brother cold and lonely in a damp hole for almost a month. And I never even said goodbye. What's it all for? I shouted, disconsolate. What's the fucking point of life? I nearly ended it all unintentionally, when I found myself staring down the front bumper of a bouncing juggernaut. Only a desperate wrench on the steering wheel saved me as it thundered past.

Days passed - weeks - without recognition. November turned into December, and what transpired in between I had no recollection. I guess it was some form of amnesia, triggered by the news. No matter: it hadn't blotted out the one event it needed to. But then how could it?

I grew resigned to the news, but inside I felt empty. I was unable to grieve - and unwilling to accept any responsibility for my absence from the funeral. My fair-weather friends I kept telling myself, they're the ones to blame. If I felt any concern for my parents it was only fleeting. I convinced myself they didn't care for me; Fergus was dead, I might as well be too for all they cared.

My lifestyle changed again. I couldn't face existence in the back of a van any more. The loneliness was all too much to bear; I needed something to occupy my mind. I decided to get a job - a proper one, preferably with long hours. Trouble was, I wasn't qualified for anything except digging holes - and I no longer fancied standing in a trench all day slinging shit over my shoulder. For the first time in my life I began to get a glimmer of what it was like to be uneducated and without ambition in society. It still didn't fully sink in though.

It was The Evening News that solved the problem. For years all I had looked at were the racing selections of B Bee, so it was a real eye-opener when I started browsing the situations vacant columns. I hadn't realised there were so many jobs in the world!

I was surprised how easy it was. Within a couple of days I had landed a job as a barman in a pub called The Ship, somewhere out Romford way. Getting the job was less difficult than getting a set of NI cards, but I forestalled any questions by saying I had just come over from Ireland.

Pulling pints wasn't too difficult a task; I had enough experience watching other people do it. And it wasn't completely alien to my nature; in the dim distant past I had helped out occasionally in the Dirty Bucket - a watering hole on the outskirts of Croagh.

I soon learned that barmen work long hours and suffer from aching feet. It wasn't just the opening hours that claimed your time; there were shelves to be stocked beforehand, glasses to be cleaned afterwards, and once a week the cellars and pipework had to be scoured clean.

A typical day began at nine in the morning and the tempo gradually built up until it reached a frenzy around lunchtime, when the whole of London seemed to need a drink for one reason or other. Then came a few hours break in the afternoon, which I spent in the local betting shop, steadily losing whatever cash I had on me.

At five thirty we opened for business again, and from then on it was more of the same until eleven when the towels were draped over the pumps. By the time the bars were cleared and we had tidied up it was midnight. Time to fall into bed. Literally. It suited me to a tee; I was busy all the time, with no opportunity to dwell on the recent past or become maudlin about things.

Even though my way of life had changed, I still couldn't resist a little fiddle on the tills. On some transactions I would under-ring a couple of shillings, and pocket the coins. It provided me with a steady twenty pounds a week - not a fortune - but also not enough to make the guv'ner suspicious.

It was Christmas before I realised it, and the festive spirit was particularly noticeable in the bar in the week leading up to it. Every evening saw a party of some kind; mini-skirted blondes competing to see who could show the most tit, numb-skull blokes vying to see who could get sick over their friends first.

Christmas day we opened the bar for a few hours in the morning. Afterwards, I sat down with the guv'ner and his wife and daughter for Christmas dinner. When the celebrations were over I felt like having a sleep so I retired to my room. I was just about to nod off on the bed when Lynne, the daughter, appeared. She began to undress.

About my age, she was a manicurist, and she sometimes helped out in the bar. She liked to rub her tits against me when the opportunity arose.

'I thought you were getting married next month', I said, as she dropped her knickers on the pile of discarded garments. It wasn't a very big pile.

'So…' she settled herself on top of me. 'I'm not going to tell, are you?'

I certainly wasn't!

Sunday afternoons in bed with Lynne became a standing order after that. In between bursts of passion she plotted the details of her forthcoming wedding to gormless Gavin. A mechanic in the employ of the Metropolitan Police, he was as thick as shit - a fact which became apparent when he and his police cronies lingered for afters on Wednesday nights. They played pontoon - a game that baboons could master - but Gavin never could grasp the finer points of the game. I failed to see his attraction for Lynne - unless it was his big dick that the others kept alluding to.

By the end of January I had grown tired of the Ship: Lynne was on honeymoon and there was little chance of 'afters' when she returned. It was time to move on.

I was now trusted by the guv'ner to the extent that he used to send me to the bank with the takings. I betrayed his trust in exemplary fashion one Monday morning when it was so cold brass monkeys were ball-less. So cold in fact that he loaned me his cashmere coat for the journey, As soon as I was out of sight of the pub I got on a bus and kept going.

That night I slept in luxury in a hotel near Baker Street, resplendent in the new clothes that I'd bought before booking in. The cashmere coat I had presented to a passing wino, which, together with a fiver, had him genuflecting in amazement.

# Chapter nine

I had fun while the money lasted. I felt a need to get away from London for a while, and for some reason headed for Clacton. There are better places than Clacton in the middle of winter! -although I enjoyed the feel of the elements in my face. It evoked memories of hilly conquests in other places. I went for long walks along the prom, climbed the headlands, admired the remnants of the bunkers and Martello towers still standing like sentinels, looking out across the bay at mainland Europe.

The snows came and racing was curtailed, so I took to playing bingo to while away the time. That this was perceived to be a woman's pastime didn't bother me; I craved excitement and it didn't matter whether it was my horse passing the post in first position or little plastic balls popping out of a drum with my numbers on them.

My sessions at the bingo hall brought me into contact with the Purdy sisters. At least they said they were sisters, but afterwards I was never quite sure. They were staying at the same hotel and we were soon on nodding terms. This must have seemed like encouragement on my part, because they were soon chatting away to me like old friends.

In the mornings, when I came down for breakfast, they would be there in the dining hall, saving a place for me at their table. They told me they were having a sabbatical from their jobs as teachers- courtesy of a legacy from some relative or other. Both were spinster types, prim and bespectacled, somewhere in their late thirties, and looked as if butter wouldn't melt in their mouths.

They didn't drink - or so I thought until the afternoon they invited me in to their room. The glass of 'something nice' turned out to be neat gin - and from the fleeting glimpse I got there seemed to be a cupboard full of it. After a couple of glasses I began to feel a little groggy, and when I looked across at one of them, seated opposite me, I realised I could see right up her dress. She was wearing no knickers! When the other sister came and sat beside her it was the same view - no knickers either! I shook my head to clear it and the spell was broken; one of them was leaning forward, offering me more gin. The offending bushes were nowhere to be seen. I put it down to hallucinations, and the following morning had almost forgotten the incident as we chatted away about such mundane topics as the weather.

The next day, when they suggested I visit them for drinks after super, I agreed. It was Janet who let me in; 'Hilly is tied up for the moment, but we won't let that stop us enjoying ourselves'.

Janet was wearing a shortie dressing gown and contrived to let it fall open as she brought me my drink. I was too nonplussed to do anything except take the drink and say, 'very nice, very nice indeed', whilst at the same time noticing that she was in no hurry to cover herself up again.

I gulped my drink down and sat on the edge of the bed. Or rather, beds. The twin beds had been pushed together to form a double. I tried to remember if it had been like that on my previous visit. No, there were definitely two beds then. I giggled to myself; twin beds for twin sisters.

Janet was hovering over me, filling my glass again, her bosoms hanging like sacks of grain. Then I heard the voice; 'Sister, sister, let me out. You promised. It's my turn now'.

It was Hilly, and the sound was coming from the wardrobe.

'Why is your sister in the wardrobe?', I found myself asking.

'She wanted to watch'. Janet marched to the wardrobe and flung it open. 'There!'

Hilly was tied up - literally. There were manacles around her hands and waist, and another running to a steel collar around her neck. Otherwise she was naked, and all I could think of was that she was definitely a bottle-blonde.

'Sister, you locked me inside', she accused.

'I did not. The door jammed. Anyway, we hadn't finished'.

We hadn't even started! And I had no intention that we should. I was feeling a bit strange, quite light-headed in fact. I shut my eyes and hoped things might have changed when I opened them again. They hadn't; the two Purdys were hovering over me like birds of prey; one blonde, one brunette, both black where it mattered. Their big tits were bouncing around in all directions, their acres of puffy flesh threatening to swamp me.

Oh, Christ, now they were pulling my trousers down, and I felt helpless to do anything about it. I felt as weak as a straw - as if I was drugged. Something cold attached itself to my dick.

'Well...?'

'Let me see now...' Hilly put her glasses on and peered at something held between my legs.

'Six...no, six and a half inches'.

'Me first...'

'No, me first.' I felt a hand cup my testicles. 'I won the toss'.

I didn't give a shit who won the toss, I wasn't hanging around any longer. I summoned my remaining strength and heaved them off me. I didn't stop running till I was safely locked inside my own room. Only then did I realise I was minus my trousers. It took me ten minutes to stop shaking. The thought of being the meat in a Purdy sandwich filled me with terror. The incident so unnerved me that I checked out the next day, hiding until the sisters had gone out.

Racing resumed shortly afterwards and I resumed my losing habits, with, fortunately, no reason to visit the bingo hall again. A few days later I did catch sight of them in the distance, a weedy specimen of manhood planted firmly between them as they strolled along the prom. Was it my imagination, or was he trying to escape?

My time in Clacton was running out; or rather my money was. I felt refreshed enough to return to NW London, where my chances of being smothered by matronly sex-maniacs were remote. A few visits to the Ace to see which way the wind was blowing informed me that Larry and Tessa had bought a house in Wembley, also that the planned business expansion had taken place. Chris was going great guns too and was planning to open another shop in Cricklewood.

I pretended indifference. But you can't wipe several years of friendship off the slate just like that, so I camouflaged my true feelings by pretending I didn't give a shit. Also, Fergus's death overshadowed everything. I wasn't willing to accept it, didn't want to believe it, so I just shut my mind and carried on as before. If I didn't think about it then it never happened.

I spent a few weeks squatting with acquaintances in a house near Queens Park station, drifting back into my previous twilight existence. However, I no longer had transport - having sold the van to raise some funds —and nobody had the flair and imagination of Larry to hustle a living out of this drudgery, so my efforts were pretty mean as a rule. I snatched a few handbags, and, once, I sat beside a woman in a betting shop with my racing paper spread across our laps, vainly searching for winners. Or at least she was; I was busy removing her purse from her handbag, which was wedged between us. Another time I sat in a photo booth, trying to open the moneybox inside, while the whole of London passed by, my OUT OF ORDER sign fooling them all.

There was an air of unreality about everything I did; almost as if I was waiting for something to happen. Perhaps I was subconsciously wanting to get caught, the act of being sent to prison removing the responsibility of having to do or think for myself. Nothing happened however, and I felt myself sinking deeper and deeper into a pit of morbidity and self-pity.

Finally, I could stand it no longer. I decided it was time to become a barman again, and I applied for a job at The Tattenham Corner House, a huge pub overlooking Epsom racecourse. It was the week before the Derby and I was amazed at the build-up in people, and fervour, as the big day drew near.

Epsom Downs itself is common land, with free access to all-and-sundry, and I watched as every 'all-and-sundry' in the land arrived and pitched his tent. The gypsies, the fortune-tellers, the three-card-trick men, the tipsters, the sword swallowers, the jugglers, the side-shows, they all came. Most of them had every thing to do with tradition and little to do with the racing. By Derby day there must have been at least a quarter of a million people on the downs.

The pub had its own problems, coping with the massive influx of people, trying to prevent the souvenir hunters from removing it piece by piece. Everything that wasn't bolted down was removed for safekeeping; come Derby day there was nothing left in the various bars except the floorboards. All the serving hatches were battened down, and drinks were served through small opening in the hatches in throwaway plastic glasses. That way the pub survived to fight another day.

It was the most hectic week I ever spent behind a bar, but by Saturday night it was all over. The doors were locked and we were preparing to throw a party to celebrate having survived the week. The manager decided not to count the tills but to leave them till the morning, and giving me the safe keys, told me to lock them away.

Opportunity had knocked again. I stuffed every pocket with notes, even my underpants and socks, then returned to the bar and asked to be excused the party as I didn't feel very well. I left the pub by a side door, walked a half mile to the nearest phone box and called a cab. Less than an hour later I was in central London.

When I counted the money in my hotel room it was over five grand, and I cursed myself for not having the presence of mind to stuff the rest of the safe's contents into a carrier bag or something. I didn't know how much I had left behind, but I knew it was more than I had taken.

A couple of days later I came across a paragraph in the Evening News with the headlines TWELVE GRAND TAKEN FROM EPSOM PUB. It was an account of my absconding, together with a reasonable description of me. Who had got the other seven grand I wondered? I shrugged, not too concerned. It was time to make myself scarce for a while.

# Chapter ten

There is something about Manchester that drives people mad. Maybe it's the constant drizzle; or maybe it's the drab sameness of row upon row of matchstick houses stretching as far as the horizon. Maybe it's just the people.

I had plumped for Mosside, and it wasn't long before the same cloud of melancholy that hung over the city descended on me. Mind you, Mosside wasn't at its best just then; a lot of it was being pulled down and it looked like a building site. Then again, some people might say it always looked like a building site.

The madness manifested itself in the form of a proposal of marriage - from me to an almost total stranger. Her name was Gina; I had barely known her two nights and there I was popping the question. She frequented the bar of the hotel where I was staying; a scruffy little dive mine host had grandly named Dicey's Nite Spot, mistakenly thinking that its gaudy walls and faded drapes gave it a bohemian look. It had more the rag-and-bone look to me, and if it drew any artists into its environs they were more likely to be piss-artists and con-artists. People like myself I suppose. However, it lured Gina and others of the hairdressing set, where they simpered and shrieked into their gin and tonics all night.

I picked up Gina the first night I put an appearance there, and from the outset she made it clear she was willing to go all the way. Almost as soon as my cock started nudging her on the darkened dance floor in fact, where she had my flies unzipped and was wanking me off before you could say 'cock-robin'. We spent most of the weekend in bed, trying to determine how much spunk I had in me. On Sunday the madness overcame me and I said we should get wed. She said why not.

On Tuesday she had a change of heart.

'I can't do it, Terry, I'm already married'.

She was sporting a black eye and other assorted bruises, the result of a thumping her old man had given her. Looking at her in daylight for the first time, I realised she was older than I thought.

'I hadn't seen him for more than a year', she sobbed. 'Since he jumped bail'.

'Where is he now?''

'In jail again. The cops got wind he was back. They took him away last night...'

She happy to see the back of him and was very loving in bed that night. I was even happier, because the wedding was off, and gave her fifty pounds to buy herself something.

-

They say that if you stand in Piccadilly long enough you will see the whole of Ireland pass by. I had always assumed this meant the one in London, not Manchester Piccadilly, so I thought I was imagining things when I saw Bannaher scuttling past in the distance. When I looked again he was disappearing through the revolving doors of a classy hotel. No doubt about it; it was him alright.

Curious, I approached the hotel. All chrome and plush carpets, and leather armchairs to get lost in.

The reception clerk confirmed my fears.

'Yes, Mr Bannaher and his party are guests here. Shall I page him for you?'

I declined, and thanked him for his help. It was only when I was outside again that the words sunk in. Bannaher and his party. Who was with him, and what were they up to in this god-forsaken hole? I decided to treat myself to a meal there, and booked a table for eight-thirty.

I arrived well beforehand and settled down in the bar to watch the comings and goings. Shortly after eight Bannaher appeared, spoke to a waiter, and was shown to a table. The bar was screened from the restaurant area so he didn't see me. The waiter returned with a drink, and after sampling it he looked at his watch and lit a cigarette, blowing little smoke-rings across his table. His mouth reminded me of a duck's arse as it opened and closed.

A few minutes later Tessa and Chris arrived. I could hear them apologising for being late. Tessa carried several bags, all of them displaying the logos of the fashion shops she had obviously been visiting. Out spending my money, I thought to myself. Her legs and arms were tanned, her face inscrutable behind a pair of dark glasses. The waiter hovered, pulled out a chair, and as she sat down and crossed her legs I caught a flash of white before her thighs clamped shut. Christ, she was still fuckable!

I looked around, expecting to see Larry following, but he was nowhere to be seen. When they went ahead and ordered, I knew he wasn't coming.

Not long afterwards I was called to my table, which proved to be adjacent to theirs. Fortified with a few drinks by now, I would cheerfully have tackled Mick McManus in the ring. I marched boldly behind the waiter.

Chris was the first to see me. In the process of spooning soup into his gob he paused, looked at me for a moment then nudged Tessa. To be fair she was cool about it. She removed her glasses, her eyes widened as she looked across, but that was her only show of emotion. Placing her spoon on the table, she wiped her lips with her napkin, a faint smile on her face.

Bannaher was still slurping away.

'Waiter,' I said, 'could you open a window? There's a terrible smell in here'.

'Sir?' the waiter, an impeccable-looking little man with an accent I couldn't place, looked worried.

'Never mind'. I laughed. 'A joke. A very little joke. Give my friends a drink. I'm sure they could do with one'.

Enlightenment flooded his face. 'Ah! Your friends'. He fluttered about. 'But you should sit with them. There is plenty of room. Besides, it is not nice to eat alone, eh?'

Tessa laughed. 'Why not?' She looked at the other two, but they didn't object. Within a minute the waiter had completed my re-location.

'No Larry?' I said as soon as I was seated. 'It would be just like old times, eh?'

'What do you want?' Chris growled.

'You invited me, remember?' The waiter arranged my cutlery in front of me. 'But since you ask, I want my money'.

Tessa looked at me with all the sincerity she could muster. 'It was stolen, Terry. Surely you don't doubt...'

'It was stolen alright. The question is by whom...'

'Now listen...' Chris began.

'Leave it'. Tessa rested her hand on his. 'It's on record, Terry. Ron Murray, Harlesden CID, that's the man you want to see if you have any doubts. Anyway, I don't see why you feel so hard done by, Larry lost just as much'.

I laughed bitterly. 'Oh yes, my old mate Larry. Where is he by the way?'

I could see eye contact between the two of them. Finally, Tessa shrugged. 'He didn't feel up to the journey. He's not feeling...too well'.

Bannaher, who had carried on slurping, now put down his spoon and pushed his plate away.

'Your friend Larry is heading for the gutter. But then, maybe he was always in it, hah?'

'We're all in the gutter...''

'...but some of us are looking at the stars...I know.' Something resembling a smile crossed his lips. 'I may not have went to school but I met the scholars, anyway'. He burped loudly. 'The thing is... he's nothing but a drunken bum...' He indicated with his head. 'They may not want to tell you, but at this moment he's drying out somewhere'.

Larry on the sauce? He liked a drink, but he couldn't have gone that much downhill so quickly.

'Fat lot of good it will do him'. He paused. 'So you feel hard done by?'

'Like I said, I want my money'.

'The landlord at the Tattenham Corner House wants his too - all twelve grand of it. But he's not going to get it, is he?'

'You shouldn't believe all you hear in the papers'.

He chuckled. 'I don't. Believe me I don't. If you got away with that amount then good luck to you. But no sermonising about what is yours eh? You never had anything that didn't belong to someone else, so don't start crying when it happens to you'.

'Is that...' I looked at Chris and Tessa...' their justification? Do unto others and all that old bollocks, but be sure to do it first?'

'You're quite it happened that way?'

'Oh for fuck sake! Do you think I was born under a cabbage or something? Of course they took the money'' I could feel the rage boiling up inside me at what he was trying to do. I would never - could never - prove they had robbed me, but I knew it just the same.

He looked pleased he had managed to needle me. 'Dishonesty is a poor bedfellow. You see treachery everywhere. Honesty is the best policy'.

I couldn't help laughing. 'And everything you've got was earned honestly?'

'I've never said it was. The difference between you and me is that I put it to good use. I make it work, give honest employment to others'

'Honest employment! The kind you gave to Johnjo and Dougie? Dougie climbs out of coffins for a living, and Johnjo is pushing up daisies for want of a bit of shuttering. Do you know what? You should be on the fucking stage'. I turned to Chris. 'What I can't understand is how you talked Larry into siding with this cowboy. He couldn't stand the sight of him. None of us could'.

'This cowboy can have you locked up before you finish your soup', Bannaher hissed before Chris could reply, 'all it takes is one phone call'. I'd never noticed the whiteness of his teeth before. 'You're not in my league now. You probably never were. No imagination is your trouble. You can't see past the next break-in, the next hold-up at some service station. You'll still be doing it in twenty years time, when you're not in jail that is'. He smiled at Tessa. 'These people have a vision of the future, that's why they're with me. They'll be raking it in; you'll still be shovelling shit. One way or another'.

'But not for you'. By Christ, not for you, you Mayo cunt!

Tessa nodded her head as their food arrived. 'Pat's right. You have the money, put it to use. Before its too late'.

Pat eh? By now I was seeing red. That smug bog-man preaching to me? I stood up. 'You remember our first meeting, Tessa? When you stole my wallet? It was too late then, only I couldn't see it. You'll always be stealing something - all of you - only you can't see it. Me? I prefer to be an honest thief'. The waiter had moved away by now. 'Tell me one thing though'.

'What's that?'

'Why did you marry Larry? And don't say love'.

She considered for a moment. 'I thought he could see the way things were going'.

'Larry can't see past the next race. Even you can't change that'. The waiter returned and placed a plate before me, but I had no stomach for it now. 'Never mind', I said, stuffing a tenner in his pocket. 'Keep the change'.

The following morning I realised I still hadn't found out what they were up to. I returned the hotel, hoping the receptionist might provide some clues.

'Mr Bannaher has already checked out', he informed me.

'And his friends?'

He wore the smirk of someone who has just pocketed a large tip.

'Miss Webster and her brother left with him'.

-

Waking up after the bender was like the aftermath of a night spent in a tumble-dryer. Dizzy, dehydrated, aching all over, I fell out of bed, straight into a pile of vomit. There was a whiskey bottle by the far wall, which I aimed erratically for. The couple of finger of spirits it contained seared the lining of my throat as it sunk like quicksilver. Soon a warm glow mushroomed upwards and did something to my brain, and I immediately felt better.

This was the third - or was it the fourth? - day of my marathon binge and it showed no signs of ending. With me, these things usually ran their course, a week being the norm, but the way I felt at the moment it could run for six months and I couldn't give a toss.

Chris and Tessa brother and sister? It didn't make sense. And yet, in a strange way, it did. The same ruthless streak was present in both of them. But why all the secrecy? I tried to remember what Tessa had said way back when we first met; her father beating her, her brother Ben nicking cars for a living. Chris had demolished the lot, saying she was a pathological liar; *'she hasn't got a brother, least not one called Ben'.*

But had she one called Chris?

My own background was just as sketchy; people in our situation just didn't tell each other their life stories. I crawled back onto the bed. Think Terry! Forget the headache and think. What was it? His mother had sent him to be reared by an aunt in Galway while she kept his sister. Half-sister? Something like that. He only learned the real truth about his mother when the aunt was dying. Shortly afterwards he'd run away to London. And tracked down Tessa?

I shook my head. It was like a story out of Peyton Place, too convoluted for my poor brain. I had always taken people at face value. Maybe that was my trouble; I was too trusting. I felt confused and hurt. We had all been friends - or so I thought. But it wasn't true, not even in the beginning. I had been the patsy right from the start.

Later, after I sobered up, I went out and began the process of getting drunk all over again. It was slow work, interspersed as it was with breaks for meals and visits to the betting shop. The betting-shop breaks were the most expensive, but they didn't stop the inexorable crawl towards that couldn't-give-a-fuck oblivion that I sought. Regular sips from the hip flask that I now carried also helped.

By evening I was rat-arsed again, and the betting shop was closing.

'Go home Paddy', the manager advised as he shoved me out. 'Tomorrow is another losing day'.

'Would you ever take a flying fuck from the highest building you can find, yeh mingy cunt'. I found myself speaking to the door. Wearily, I drew back my foot to kick the obstruction off its hinges.

As luck would have it, Gina came round the corner at that moment and saved my bacon. She hailed a passing taxi and got me away in one piece. She must have got me back to the hotel in one piece, because my next memory was of waking up in my room, shivering. I was naked, and without bedclothes covering me. I switched on the light, and finding the eiderdown on the floor, wrapped it round me, then looked at my watch. Twelve thirty. Too late for a drink in the bar. Of my hip-flask there was no sign. I had to have something;

there was a furnace in my throat that needed dowsing. Then I remembered the kitchen; I had seen a bottle of something there. Still wrapped in the eiderdown, I made my way along the corridor and switched on the kitchen light. Cooking sherry; that would have to do Moments later I was back in my room, the sickly sweet juice gurgling down my throat.

By one-o-clock I was paralytic again. I couldn't lie down; the room rocked violently if I did, and if I closed my eyes I had this sensation of falling, falling, falling...

I tried sitting upright but it wasn't much better. I tried walking, but that also proved difficult; my legs wouldn't go where I pointed them. In the end I found that standing stationary in a corner of the room was the best way to die. I was holding on for dear life when the window began rattling.

'Terry, Terry, let me in'.

Getting to the window proved more difficult than I anticipated, getting it open even more so. Mosside looked even shittier in the dim night light; there was a damp mist hanging over the mean streets that gave it an eerie, dead appearance. I could see a face in front of me - two faces even? - that looked vaguely familiar.

'You can't stay out there', I slurred. 'The entrance is....is...' Where the fuck was the entrance?...' over there somewhere'.

'It's locked you berk'. I felt a hand shove at me. 'That's why I'm coming in the window'. Then I was sitting on the floor and Gina was sitting beside me

'You've got a black eye', I began to laugh, 'you've got two black eyes'. Then I was singing. 'Two lovely black eyes...two lovely black eyes...'

I got a dig in the stomach that knocked all the wind out of me. 'Quiet, you drunken bastard or you'll wake the whole of Mosside'. She winced. 'Yeah, I've got two black eyes. And a couple of bruised ribs. That no-good husband of mine was let out on bail again. He's going to skip again, and he's sent me out to get some money for him'.

'Money doesn't grow on trees', I said stupidly.

'Nor on bedroom carpets. What d'ya think I'm doing here? ' There were tears in her eyes. I can't do it. I can't go and....you know'. She wiped her eyes. 'I was hoping you might let me have some...'

'Tessa asked me for money once. When I didn't give it to her she took it anyhow. All women are whores...' I could feel the contents of my stomach surging...'I think I'm going to be sick'.

'Oh Jesus!' She leaped away as I spewed up between my legs. 'Are you going to let me have it?'

'Have what?'

'The money'.

'Come back next week…when…I'm…sober', I managed between retches.

'Tonight…I need it tonight'.

'I need it tonight too, I grinned stupidly at her. 'But I don't think I can manage it…' I let the eiderdown fall away and tried to leer. 'Do you think you could…?'

'You drunken fuckpig'. She slapped my hand away in disgust. 'I'd rather give a blow-job to a gorilla'. She stood up. 'Forget it…forget I asked you for anything'. Then she was gone, back through the window.

I saw her picture of her a few days later in the local paper. She had been found strangled in her flat by police, who had come looking for her husband. They were now looking for him in connection with her murder. Poor Gina, her choice in men-folk left something to be desired. I wasn't excluding myself from that assessment.

I began drinking more heavily, gambling more stupidly than ever before. Oddly enough, I didn't lose much more quickly, and as the weeks dragged into months I was still hanging in there. Teetering on the brink of disaster, but never quite making it.

Subconsciously, I must have had a desire to end the deception, end all the cheating and stealing. Gradually, there came a realisation that what I was doing, the kind of life I was living, was no life at all. It wasn't even an existence.

I had no friends, no family, no convictions, no nothing. I didn't really believe in anything anymore. And I began to envy those who had something they could fight for. Some cause they would go to the ends of the earth for. Some principle they would die for.

What would I fight for? What would I die for? I shook my head. Sweet fuck-all. Nothing was worth it. I was a rebel alright, but one without a cause.

Eventually, I was almost broke again, spending my days cooped up in my room, trying to come to terms with myself. If I had given Gina the money would she be alive now? What good was money? What good had it done me? I told myself that I could get a job in another bar. But what then? Do another bunk with the takings? And repeat it for the rest of my life? Naw, fuck that for a game of soldiers.

Giving myself up proved to be more difficult than I expected. I could have walked to a police station I suppose, but I didn't know of one offhand, so I just found the nearest phone-booth and gave myself up over the phone.

It seemed to take an age; they wanted details of the crimes I'd committed, saying they couldn't just take my word for it. Could I ring back in half an hour?

The second time I phoned they asked if I still had the money.

'What do you think?' I asked.

Three Panda cars eventually turned up and swooped on me as if I was an escaped prisoner. I got my first and only glimpse of Old Trafford as we headed for a downtown police cell.

# Chapter eleven

Dublin didn't particularly smile on this returning prodigal. Not that I ever expected much from this quarter; if you didn't possess a Dublin accent you were handicapped straight away. Oh yes, the Jackeens looked after their own. If I'd worn a card saying 'plague' I couldn't have been made less welcome. Ever since I had been dumped at the airport with my miserable bundle of belongings the smiles on the face of officialdom had merely glared at me from a safe distance. Cead Mile Failte my arse!

Pathetic, I said to myself. Five years. Five long fucking years and what is there to show for it? The returning hero is back in town - and with less to his name than when he left. I had ten shillings in my pocket, a rumbling in my stomach, and not a notion of how to get from the airport to the city. Some fucking homecoming!

Dejected, I made my along the Dublin road in the pouring rain. Eventually, a city-bound trucker took pity on me. He was the silent type, thank Christ —I couldn't have stomached another Derek. I spent the night skulking in Connolly Station, scavenging for food, competing with the homeless dogs. I knew how they felt.

Early in the morning I managed to stow away on the mail-train heading south. I finished my journey in a coal-delivery lorry, having hitched a ride from the railway station in Waterford. It took numerous stops for deliveries and refreshments before I was within walking distance of home.

Seeing it gave me a shock. Where once it was trim and comforting, now it looked neglected. The privet hedges, usually trimmed with spirit-level exactness, laboured untidily upwards and outwards. The whitewashed piers and walls were flaking and discoloured, and the flowerbeds, once a mass of foliage and colour, were now a wasteland of thistles and dock weed. Even the cats looked scruffy.

Mother didn't seem too surprised to see me, nor was she too excited either. I had written to tell her of my impending arrival, so perhaps that was the reason.

'Your father had a wee stroke', were her first words to me.' He's in hospital'. She took a letter from her apron and waved it at me. 'Just as well and all. I don't know what he'd say if he saw this'. I could see the words HM PRISON stamped across the top of it.

'That's all behind me now, mum', I said. I meant it too. I'd had lots of time to think in the past year. I would get a job, turn over a new leaf. Revenge could wait.

She harrumphed a bit, but I could see she was pleased. She seemed smaller somehow; there was less of her than when I had last seen her; it was as if the passage of time had diminished her. With a start, I realised she was nearly sixty. She didn't look that old, but I could see the grey hair, and the crinkles round her eyes and mouth. The tears welled in my eyes; I wanted to hold her, hug her... but somehow I couldn't.

'You'd better take Fergus's room', she said.

Fergus's room! All my childhood was spent in that room. It was just as much my room as his. We had even slept in the same bed until he'd grown too big. Lying there in the dark, listening to the wind and the rain, one whistling through the pine grove outside, the other dancing on the window-panes, I felt safe. It was my haven against the bogey man and the mayor's dog, and all the other inhabitants of the cruel and frightening world of adults. The one place, where, if I pulled the bedclothes up over my ears, nothing could touch me. To hear it referred to as Fergus's room hurt.

'Poor Fergus', my mother said.

I had done all my grieving for Fergus. Nothing was going to bring him back. Guilt was something else though. Guilt at missing his funeral. I would have given anything to put things right, but I knew he would understand. At least I hoped he would. He didn't have much truck with solemn occasions; give him the flowers when he was living he'd always said, they were no good to you dead.

'Yes', I replied, 'poor Fergus. I'll put some flowers on his grave tomorrow'. She wouldn't understand if I'd said anything else.

That seemed to cheer her up. 'His motorbike is still in the shed. I suppose it's yours now. He always said he wanted you to have it'.

I'd forgotten about the bike. Forgotten about the joy, the sense of freedom a bike brings. I had owned a small Honda before I left for England, but it was a midget compared to this Triumph. Later in the day I sampled its power, finding myself almost airborne on several occasions before getting the hang of it.

Later still, I tried to find out the extent of father's illness. Not life-threatening, the hospital said when I phoned. Nevertheless a reminder to slow down. When I suggested visiting him visiting him, mother refused point blank. Then I remembered she had an irrational fear of hospitals; something to do with when she was young and had almost died of typhoid fever. Her experiences in the fever ward still gave her nightmares.

'He'll be home in a few days', she said. 'He'll just have to take things easy. I thought retirement might slow him down.'

With a shock, I realised he was sixty six, past retirement age. All his life a working man, and nearly forty years of it spent humping bags of feedstuffs at Crotty's Mills. My inheritance, if I followed his path.

'I suppose it's the Hill?' The Hill was his tenuous claim to being a land owner. And it wasn't even a complete hill, merely one face of it, the other, larger, portion being part of the Faulkner farm, which lay on its far side. His total holding was eight acres. Four of them formed the Hill, the remainder comprised two stony meadows at the foot of it.

For as long as I could remember, he had nurtured that hill, clearing it bit by bit, removing stones, seeding it. It still remained a wilderness; no matter how many stones we removed, the next year more had appeared. It was as if they grew there annually.

When we were young, Ritchie Faulkner and myself regarded the Hill as our own personal playground. It was there we fought The Battle Of The Boyne, The War Of The Worlds, The Siege Of Troy, The Alamo; rode bareback, side-saddle and shotgun; played Tarzan, Tonto and the Devil himself. In short, we lived and breathed the Hill.

There was a small cave near the top, on Faulkner's side, which we used as a hide-out, and from where we would watch the goings-on in the village below. In the summer evenings, at weekends, there was open-air dancing on a stage in the narrow field opposite the pub, where, from our vantage point, we listened to the whoops of joy and the thump of leather on timber ripping through the warm evening, and aped the performers with our own version of the dancing. In the autumn the travelling shows came and pitched their tents, and the stage was covered over and used by actors and singers.

One evening we found our cave occupied by Ritchie's older brother, Jafe, and Molly Carey, a young woman whose husband had gone to Birmingham to look for work. Jafe beat the living daylights out of us and warned us not to tell anyone. It was never quite the same afterwards.

'The Hill is your father's life. He won't change now'.

'If he doesn't…' I didn't finish. 'He'll have to change, that's all there's to it'.

'You could help him'.

As if he'd let me.

'It's a hill, mother. What can you do with a hill?'

'It's all he has left'.

'It'll kill him. The way it did grandad'. My paternal grandfather had keeled over one day on top it, fracturing his skull on a jagged stone. I was ten at the time, and had watched from my perch on a rock in one of the meadows as he came tumbling down. He had rolled some of the way, coming to a rest against a boulder, his wooden leg breaking away from his body before he came to a stop. I could still picture the leg, laying like a lump of driftwood in his wake.

'It wasn't the Hill that killed your grandfather'.

She was right of course. But it was easier to apportion the blame to a lump of rock than it was to drink. The demon drink, he called it. But it was a term of endearment more than anything else;

Oh moonshine, dear moonshine, how I loved thee
You killed my poor father but you won't kill me
I'll eat in the morning, and I'll drink when I'm dry
And if moonshine don't kill me I'll live till I die.

That he was wrong - and knew he was wrong - didn't bother him in the least. He always maintained he was living on borrowed time anyway. By his reckoning he number should have been called in the slaughter-house that was Flanders Fields, where, if the British officers had had their way, he would have lost his head rather than his leg;

'They forced us out of the trenches at gunpoint. If it hadn't been a lump of German shrapnel it would have been a British bullet. Do you know what keeps France's fields so green? Thousands of tons of human fertiliser - the best manure in the world'.

He was the recipient of a small Army pension, which he supplemented by making poteen in the hills behind Croagh. Sadly, he had been one of his own best customers. The pathologist who carried out the post mortem said he would have been dead in a few months regardless, as his liver had almost rotted away.

Father, on the other hand, perhaps fearful of becoming what his father was, hardly ever drank, and refused to assist in any way in the making of the poteen. The result was that Grandad had spent most of his time either up in the hills, or working at the Faulkner's farm, where the young Jafe and Ritchie idolised him. It was understandable in a way; he sang songs and told stories, and generally kept them amused, all of which lessened their grief at the loss of their father in a drowning accident at their quarry.

The day after my return I walked the half mile to Croagh Cross, to buy some bread for mother. The Croagh Road we called it, although it was little more than a glorified boreen, its ditches so close together it was difficult for cars to pass each other. Tall trees overhung much of it, overlapping in places, so that it was permanently in shade.

Croagh itself was a collection of ramshackle buildings nestling in what was grandiosely called the Croagh Valley. There was the pub, a thatched affair that also sold bread and groceries; the Creamery, the church and graveyard, and on the outskirts, hidden behind a grove of pine trees, the school. A few whitewashed cottages made up the remainder of the village. Most of the buildings were old and dilapidated, the exception being the school, which had been built after the war.

The outlying land was mostly scrub where it wasn't hilly, and those who tried to eke out a living found themselves cursing and praying with equal sincerity. Behind our hill were larger hills and more valleys, and behind them mountains, hence the concoctions of icy rain and mists that frequently swept down over Croagh, lashing across the plains before disappearing out to sea half a dozen miles in the other direction.

As I passed the school I saw that the burnt-out classroom had been replaced. My one regret was that I hadn't done the job properly. If I had learnt anything from that academy of useless information, it was the Master's motto; 'do it right the first time'.

Passing the church I knew I had to see Fergus's grave. I had only a vague idea where the family plot was and it took some time to find. When I finally located it and saw Fergus's name carved on the slab of grainy marble I couldn't stop the tears coming. It was the first time I had cried since hearing the news and it was several minutes before I could stem the flow. Even then the sight of his age - 30 YEARS OLD - had me sniffling again. Thirty years of age; what had he got out of life? What had it all been for?

'I thought it was you, Terence'.

I hadn't heard Fr Maguire come up behind me. I felt embarrassed at my crying and tried to hide my tears.

'Shedding tears is the emotional safety-valve that the Lord in his infinite wisdom has seen fit to provide. Never be afraid to cry'.

'I wish I had been here, 'I heard myself say. 'It was so unfair, such a waste'.

'Nobody ever promised us that life would be fair. The best we can do - any of us - is try to lead good lives, and always be prepared for the Lord's call'.

'I know Fr. Suffer little children to come unto me, and the meek shall inherit the earth...isn't that how it goes?' I couldn't keep the bitterness out of my voice.

'Don't be too hard on yourself''.

'What do you mean?'

'I think we both know the answer to that. Your anger isn't against Our Lord, it's against yourself'.

'I should have been here'.

He nodded sympathetically. 'You loved your brother'. This was a statement. 'And I'm sure that whatever kept you from being here, he will understand. Pray for his soul, that's all he asks'.

I began to walk away, unable to dwell on it any longer. 'I never knew, not until weeks later. Not until it was too late...'

He followed, making placatory noises, but I hardly heard. Finally, by the church gate, a name registered.

'Bannaher? Did you say Bannaher?'

'I was merely commenting on his generosity'. His hand waved in the general direction of the church. 'Brand new as you can see...'

I realised he had been talking about the sacristy roof, which, as I now saw, had been newly slated. At least Dougie's exertions hadn't been totally wasted...

'A generous man', he continued. 'The sort of man that is the backbone of the community. Indeed we should consider ourselves fortunate, as I believe there is every chance of him coming to live here...'

'In Croagh!' I could hardly believe my ears.

'Not too far away. Ross-On-Sea. He's in the construction business I believe, and he sees development potential there'.

The construction business? A fucking subby... the lowest of the low. The shit on my boot, that's what he was. It was too much for me. I made some excuse to get away and headed for the pub. Bannaher in London I could just about suffer, Bannaher in my own back yard was a fucking nightmare.

-

The interior of the Dirty Bucket hadn't changed one bit for as long I could remember. Stone floors cold to the touch even on the warmest day, wainscoting and ceiling sickly-looking with nicotine stains, the half-nets on the windows yellowing and torn. A faded mirror advertising PADDY WHISKY hung over the fireplace, and the fire itself gave off a pungent aroma from the sods of turf blazing in the hearth.

'Take a good look at it, boy. You won't be seeing it for much longer'.

'Ritchie!' I turned around as the familiar voice spoke.

We shook hands warmly then he placed a large brandy in front of me. I downed it in one gulp.

'I needed that'.

He laughed heartily, a shock of tousled blond hair falling over his eyes as he did so. He swept it back with his hand, his slate-blue eyes twinkling as he grinned at me.

'I heard you were back. You should have let me know you were coming and I would have rolled out the red carpet. If I had a red carpet'

'I already got the treatment in Dublin'. He arched his eyebrows and I continued. 'It's a long story. I'll tell it to you sometime you have a few weeks to spare'. I looked around. 'You behind a bar? I'd never have believed it. I thought you'd be in Kookaburra, or wherever, by now'.

When we were young he'd always talked about working in the Australian outback. He got the idea, I knew, from watching a film we'd seen in the Fishermen's Hall in Ross-On-Sea once. The film had featured a sheep-shearing sequence, where a line of contestants battled the clock, shearing their sheep in some ridiculously short time.

He grinned again. 'I'm behind the bar because I own it. Uncle Tom died last year and left it to me'. He waved his hand at the interior. 'I meant what I said about not seeing this for much longer. Come summer you won't recognise the place'.

'What about the name?'

'The Dirty Bucket'.

'Ah Jaysus, you can't!'

'Why not? Sure isn't that what everybody calls it already'.

Although the sign over the door said FAULKNERS BAR, it had been known as The Dirty Bucket for longer than I could remember. Its unofficial name had come about after the big freeze of '47, when Ritchie's grand-uncle, its then owner, had placed buckets at strategic points throughout the bar for the customers to relieve themselves without having to go outside in the cold. The custom had lingered for years, until the health authorities told him it would have to cease. 'Talk about having a piss-up in a brewery', Fergus had once said, 'it was more like having a pint in a cess-pit'.

'And Jafe...how is he?'

'We're civil to each other...the odd time we meet'. His voice was stark.

89

'He doesn't drink here, then?' Then I remembered Jafe didn't drink. He never had. His passion was hurling; he believed that the search for excellence in sport was best pursued with a body free from the abuses of alcohol. He was good at it too, having already won an All-Ireland medal for his efforts. Hurling was also Ritchie's passion. But he was not in Jafe's league. Still good nevertheless; a tough uncompromising player who broke more than his fair share of camans during a game.

'You planning to stay around?' Ritchie poured another shot of Hennessey.

'Only as long as it takes me to shake the dust from my clothes'. I laughed. 'I think I've already outstayed my welcome'.

The next day that departure became more pressing. Father had come home from hospital and was monosyllabic to my questions. Still, even a grunt was an improvement on the past. He didn't seem to have any questions of his own, and there were times when I caught him looking at me with a puzzled look on his face. Try as I might, I could feel any real resentment towards him. He was an old man, battered into his hunched-up posture by the harshness of his life, not the ogre I had made him out to be. When I looked at his weather-beaten face, his hair sparse and ivory-white, I saw my own reflection. This would be me in forty years time if I stayed.

Sergeant Cronin speeded up my departure a bit more. I had been taking a ride on the Triumph, and had been drawn by curiosity to stop and watch the activities at Jafe's farm. Several machines were beavering away at the base of the hill, one of them stopping every now and then to load a tractor and trailer. I decided to wait for the tractor to make its way back to the road and ask what was going on, not noticing that the Sergeant had pulled up beside me.

He climbed from his car. 'Have you got tax and insurance for that machine?' he asked, circling the bike several times. 'I don't suppose you have', he continued before I could answer. ''Let me give you some advice, lad. I know where you've been, and I know you're back now, but don't let the grass grow under your feet. You know what I'm saying?' He stopped circling and looked at me. 'You see my problem? Every time there's trouble - a break-in or a robbery- I'll wind up asking myself 'is it him?' And even if it's not, I won't ever be sure. It'll be trouble for me, trouble for you, and worst of all, trouble for your poor father and mother. D'you see what I'm getting at? We don't want your sort around here'.

I felt like asking him what my sort was. But I knew what he meant.

'I have no notion of staying around this fucking dump', I replied.' I can't wait to get away again'.

As he was pulling away the tractor passed by. It was laden down with sand.

# Chapter twelve

The scene was like one from a bad cowboy film. The Deegan clan, all three of them, had their enemy surrounded. They had formed a semi-circle and were now pointing an array of weapons at the bewildered workmen.

The father was pointing a double-barreled shotgun in the direction of the digger-driver. The driver had alighted from his cab and was standing by the trench with his hands in the air. The older of the sons was brandishing an axe, which, although blunted along its cutting edge, could still quite easily split a skull. The youngest boy, about fifteen and gangly as a foal, stood his ground, a pitchfork clenched in his hands.

Curiously, the first thing that came into my mind was that none of them wore wellingtons. I had always associated farmers with shit and muck and wellies, but it was the workmen who were wearing the latter. Nobody moved as a battered jeep came speeding towards us.

'What the fuck is going on here?' Moynihan roared, jumping from the jeep as it scattered stones indiscriminately.

'John Wayne here thinks he owns the countryside', the digger driver lowered his hands.

'He does. Most of it around these parts anyway'. Moynihan looked at Deegan. 'Why are you stopping my men from working?'

'Their work is it?' The old farmer spat the words then fixed his cap so that the peak was pointing over his left ear. 'Is it their work to knock down my fences and flatten a quarter acre of turnips every time that machine turns round?'

I could see the inroads the driver had made into the turnip field. I knew it had been deliberate; he'd been annoyed at Deegan's bossy interference with the work; *you can't do that, you can't go there...I'll show the ould bastard what I can do'*.

'I'm sorry about your turnips', Moynihan said. 'I'll see you're compensated. Now, stop pointing that thing at people, it might go off''.

'It's not loaded'. He lowered it to his side, then raised it again, jabbing it in the driver's direction. 'Just make sure he keeps to the agreed boundaries, is all...or next time it might be'. He inclined his head at the sons and they all turned on their heels and headed up the shingle driveway that led to the farmyard.

'That's one mad ould hoor', one of the ground crew remarked, as we watched them retreat. 'I remember one time he dragged a huntsman from his horse and threatened to rip his gizzards out with his pitchfork'.

'What for?'

'They were hunting on his land. Oh yes, he's mighty touchy about his land'.

Further conversation was cut short by Moynihan's bellow; *why the fuck were we standing about when there was work to be done!*

I had been part of this pipe-laying gang for several weeks now, and was beginning to quite like the idea of working for a living. My job was welding the pipes together before they were laid in the trench and the ground made good in our wake. The idea was to leave the land as we found it, but in many cases we made improvements, new gates and fencing replacing old and broken ones. The pipeline ran between Cork and Limerick, and would eventually carry the natural gas that was currently being extracted from the North Sea.

-

I had answered an ad in a newspaper and travelled to Limerick to be interviewed for the job. The lies on my application form didn't raise any eyebrows in the site manager's office; he scanned my completed form impassively, nodding every now and again, then sent for Moynihan and told him to give me a welding test. That I had passed was mainly due to the foreman's desire to get away early for a pint. He watched me only long enough to confirm that I could stick two bits of metal together, before telling me I had the job.

On site it was a different story. I hadn't done much pipe welding on the training course in jail, and when he saw my first efforts he roared; 'I thought you could fucking weld! I've seen goat-shit look better than that'. It was only now that I was getting the hang of it.

I was billeted with a dozen others in two adjoining houses in a sleepy street not far from the docks area of the city. The company, based in Manchester, had brought over a number of skilled workers, and had acquired the houses so that accommodation wouldn't be a problem. There had been rumblings of discontent amongst the local trades unions at the lack of jobs for local men, so perhaps my employment was a kind of olive branch.

Moynihan explained in more detail one evening in Jango's Tavern, a side-street dive not too far from our digs. Jango's chief rival in the decibel stakes was a motorcycle shop a few doors away; if heavy rock music from the jukebox wasn't pounding your ears, then the staccato beat of engines revving up and backfiring ricocheted through the narrow lane.

'We're walking a thin line', he said. 'A local company was supposed to have the contract in their pocket, but we greased a few palms. Slipped in the back way as it were. 'Course, we had to honour an agreement to take on more locals…'

'I'm not exactly a local'.

'No., but you're more fucking local than those Scousers and Geordies back there in camp. And all the labourers are local, which helps. But with all the bad feeling going down there's bound to be a few trouble-makers among them'. He looked at me. 'There's a fella called Tom Whyte. Ever meet him?'

I shook my head.

'The last word I heard, he had to get out of London in a hurry. Something about some demolition explosives going missing'.

'Why take him on then?'

'That's it, we didn't'. Some of the work is subbed out, he got in that way'.

Inside the Cavern the world was mostly black; black ceilings, black furniture, black floor. The walls were white, and were adorned by unframed canvasses, mainly daubed with splashes of vivid red, blue and orange. It was as if the artist had stood back and hurled the paint at them. The long bar was lit by a surrealist glow, eerily bright against the dark surrounding, effected, it seemed, by strategic positioning of coloured strip-lighting.

Its owner was a soft-spoken Englishman from Devon known only as Jango. He wore tiny round-frame glasses of high magnification, so that his eyes looked like tennis balls behind the lenses. The paintings on the walls were his handiwork, though his speciality was steel sculptures, made mainly from bits of metal salvaged from the city's scrap-yards. One room of the pub had been converted to a studio/workshop, where his work was on display. He was also an occasional poet, his offerings often bawled out from the tiny stage in a corner of the bar to his usually bewildered customers. More often than not he was high on Guinness and Ganja.

''Did you see the cut of the stuff he makes?' Moynihan asked me on my second or third visit there. 'Works of art, me arse! Every time I look at one of them all it reminds me is of one dog riding the hole off another dog'.

I had to admit that was true. All were of animals of one shape or another, all were in pairs, and one was usually on the back of the other.

'Can you see any Limerick man, or woman for that matter, with something like that decorating the mantelpiece?

'Ah now, they're not all bogmen'.

'Is it codding me you are?'

I couldn't stop laughing. 'Too sophisticated I suppose'.

'Sophisticated my arse! It's all about mentality. Don't you know all Englishmen are obsessed with their holes? Always trying to get up each others. And their women's. It might be alright for those shirt-lifters in the wilds of Devon or wherever, but I can't see it catching on here'.

Tonight, the stage was occupied by a trio of musicians. The singer was female, pink-lipped and sheathed in black from neck to toe. She sang a song about love and the loss of innocence in a voice rich in inflection, inclining her body forward as she sang. Predatory was the word that came to mind. An uillean piper accompanied her, his eyes closed, whilst the third member used his guitar to keep the tempo going. I thought she was terrific.

During the session Moynihan nudged me.

'That's Whyte come in now'.

I looked over to the far end of the bar. Whyte's lank, shiny black hair fell across his face as he looked at us. His eyes were like steel ball-bearings in their sockets, cold and grey, the sliver of moustache under his nose looking like a pencil mark. He lifted his glass in our direction then downed its contents.

'Some people are particular who they drink with', he said loud enough for us to hear, then left.

I soon forgot the incident because the singing session finished and Jango was introducing me to the songbird.

'This is Jennifer. Be careful what you say, she's also a reporter'.

'I also play football and climb mountains', she laughed. 'And I ride a motorbike'.

'That's a couple of things we have in common, then'.

She shook her hair free then pushed it behind her ears. I couldn't see a ring on any finger.

'Let me guess. You're not a reporter anyway'. She studied me for a moment. 'I'd say motorbikes and mountain climbing'.

'The bike bit was easy'. I indicated my jacket. 'But what made you pick mountain climbing'.

'All the fellas I know who play football have muscular thighs. You haven't'.

'I have been compared to a stick-insect once or twice. But never so diplomatically'.

She laughed again. 'I didn't mean it like that. You're more...streamlined'.

By now Moyhihan had slipped away and Jango had gone behind the bar. I bought her a drink and we adjourned to a corner.

She was in her early or mid twenties I guessed. The skin on her face was smooth and peachy looking; the only blemish a beauty-spot low down on her left cheek. But perhaps it wasn't an imperfection; it could just as easily have been placed there by a pencil.

'Which is the real you, singer or reporter?'

She shrugged. 'I can be both, can't I? Why make a straightjacket for myself when I don't have to? Someday I'll have to make the choice, but till then...' she sipped her Bacardi and smiled at me.

'I can't believe your writing is better than your singing, so perhaps the choice is already made'.

'Maybe'. She continued smiling. 'You're not from Limerick?'

I shook my head.

'From London?'

'Only by way of spending a few years there. Ever heard of a place called Croagh?'

Now it was here turn to shake her head.

'Not many have'. I waved my hand. 'Out there, over the hills, that's where my home is'.

'Is it?'

I couldn't help laughing. 'Not really. I was born there, but I wouldn't call it home anymore'.

'Oh, you poor homeless soul, wandering the cities of the world. And what is it that brings you to Limerick?'

'The peace and quiet of Croagh was driving me mad. Give me the bright city lights any day of the week'.

'I imagine the London lights are a lot brighter than the ones on display here'.

'They are'.

'So why are you here when you could be there?'

I shrugged. 'We can't always have what we want'.

'Why do I sense a story behind that remark?'

'You nose, I suppose'.

'What's wrong with my nose?'. She looked crestfallen

'Nothing', I added hastily. 'It's just an expression...'Then I saw that she was laughing at me...'but you're right. I might even tell you about it sometime'.

She finished her drink and stood up. 'I'd like that'. Then she named the paper she worked for.

'You can get hold of me there most days'.

After she had left a feeling of intense loneliness welled up inside me. She was right; London was my city. For all its imperfections it was the place I longed to be, the place where the people I could identify with dwelled. Limerick was just a conglomeration of concrete and steel to me; a maze of poor housing and crumbling buildings. Where young women carrying babies wrapped in their shawls begged openly in the streets; where down-and-outs high on red biddy cluttered shopways, shouting abuse at passers-by; and prostitutes offered migrant workers like myself blow-jobs for a fiver behind the warehouses on the dockside.

I had already seen most of what the city had to offer, walking its streets in the evenings before the pubs beckoned. Southill, where the tinkers lived in caravans and kept their animals in the houses allocated to them by the council, and where young men rode ponies bare-back along the roads like modern-day Geronimo's. Thomondgate, part of the old city, slowly crumbling into the Shannon; said to be the spot where the horses carrying John Scanlon, the murderer of the Colleen Bawn, stopped and refused to go any further. Scanlon, it is said, got out and walked to his execution at Gallows Green, on the Clare side of the river, head held high, declaring from the gallows that he was innocent.

Then there was Sarsfield's Ride.

'Do you know of Sarsfields Ride?' Moynihan asked me one evening.

'No. Is she any good?'

'Sarsfield's Ride, you prick, the route Patrick Sarsfield took when he waylaid an ammunition train of King Willie's that was headed for the city to blow it to smithereens'.

'Oh that? I thought you were referring to one of those scrubbers down the docks'

He shook his head. 'You're a waste of space, boy. You know fuck all about welding - and less about history!'

'I know plenty about King Wullie; He kicked the shit out of King James and his army at the battle of the Boyne then rampaged through the country, leaving a trail of death and destruction behind him. James deserted his men and fecked off back to France, leaving Sarsfield to make the best of things. Afterwards, when Limerick was under siege and about to receive an almighty battering from Wullies' heavy artillery train, which was being brought in from Cashel, Sarsfield got wind of it. He, and a group of his men, aided by a guide named Galloping Hogan, rode through the night, across Keeper Mountain, and ambushed the convoy at Balyneety, blowing the lot to kingdom come'.

Moynihan laughed. 'Well, by Christ, now there's an eye-opener! If you didn't go to school itself, you surely met the scholars. Here, have another one'.

I had another one, and then a few more after that, and before I went to bed that night I made a mental note to ask Jennifer if she fancied following in Sarsfield's footsteps. On our bikes of course.

# Chapter thirteen

It didn't take Tom Whyte long to make an impact. A week after he started work he broke the jaw of one of the crane drivers. I, for one, wasn't too put out; he was a flash Geordie who had it coming.

'The stupid prat was flying a Union Jack on his jib', Moynihan told me later that night. 'Whyte spotted it and dragged him from his cab. There was a fight and he busted his jaw'.

'There's your chance to get rid of him. Union or no union...'

'Too risky. There's a lot of nationalist feeling around these parts. And it might be what he wants. Anything to cause a strike'.

'I don't understand that driver. He's a flash bastard, but he's not stupid. I mean...a Union Jack...'

Moynihan snorted. 'He swears he didn't put it there'.

'D'you believe him?'

'As you say, he can't be that stupid. Still, I can't afford to take a chance. He's got his ticket back to Geordie-land tomorrow'.

The following day, Whyte turned up in our area, renewing some fencing. I watched as he hammered timber posts into the ground, using a heavy metal driver. This he lifted in both hands by its ears then dropped on the post a dozen times or so in rapid succession, each blow sinking the post a little bit more. Heavy, physical work; not for the faint-hearted or the hung-over. A youth, tall and blonde, lounged close-by him, smoking and chatting as he worked.

After a while, Whyte looked over. 'You'll know me next time'.

'I was just curious'.

'You know what curiosity did to the cat'. He laughed at his little joke. 'What are you curious about?

'About what made you break that driver's jaw?'

He turned to the youth.

'Do you hear that, Jimmy? There's a fine patriot for you'. He turned back to me. 'If I had stuck a Tricolour on a pole on a building site in London, how long do you think I would have lasted? A damn sight less than he did. That's why I broke his jaw. And then I burned his fucking flag'. He turned to Jimmy again. 'Burn everything British 'cept their coal, eh Jimmy?'

Jimmy thought that was hilarious. 'Oh, that's a good one, Tom. Burn everything British except their coal. I must make a note of that'.

'Who's he - your stooge?'

'Jimmy?' He punched the other affectionately. 'He's my assistant, aren't you Jimmy? Except he's not much good at it'.

Jimmy tapped his forehead. 'I get dizzy spells whenever I lift anything heavy'.

'Or anything light'.

'Or anything light', agreed Jimmy

'You keep strange company', said Whyte when they had finished laughing.

'I don't follow you'.

'The other night, in the Cavern. Fraternising with the enemy'.

I had to think for a moment. 'Moynihan the enemy? Give over. He's been on the tools all his life. He only took this job to get away from the missus'.

'All the same, he'll have to take side when the revolution comes'.

'What fucking revolution? It's only a bloody job'.

He drove the last of the posts home then threw his tools into the back of the pick-up. 'We'll have to pick up some more posts in the yard, Jimmy', he said, tossing a bunch of keys at him. As he climbed over the tailboard he shouted at me. 'There's always a revolution. The secret is to be on the right side when it comes'.

-

Ritchie Faulkner had begun his modernization programme the next time I visited home. Half the thatch had already been removed, and new walls were rising which, when complete, would swallow up most of the old building. All that would eventually be recognisable as the old house would be its front entrance.

'Never do anything by halves', he said to me. 'Sure, I could have spent a few thousand cleaning it up, but what would be the point? You still couldn't swing a cat inside. When it's finished it will be somewhere people will want to come to for a night out. Good food, music, a place to bring the wife or girlfriend'.

'Or the mistress'.

He laughed. 'Uncle Tom never made more than enough to keep himself alive. The reason he never married, he said, was because he couldn't afford it. I'm not falling into that trap. Depending on the likes of Jafe for a living. The farmers of this parish would see you starve before they'd spend a few bob'. He rolled up the plans he'd been showing me. 'Ritchie's Road House won't be beholdin' to any of them'.

'Why do I have this feeling you know something?'

'I'm banking on the future prosperity of Croagh. It took me some time to convince the bank manager, but in the end I did it. I think what swung it is yer man that just bought Ross House. There's talk of him building a holiday complex over there'.

.He's not called Bannaher by any chance?'

'That's the fella. Said to have banked a million selling his business in England'.

If he'd sold up there must be a good reason for it. Probably the taxman - I couldn't see him walking away from easy money voluntarily.

Before I left I paid a visit to Ross House. A big, leafy estate on the outskirts of Ross-On-Sea, it had been owned in my youth by a reclusive Englishman who guarded his privacy with warning notices, barbed-wire fences, and a couple of Dobermans as big as donkeys. I had read somewhere that there had been several attempts in recent years to burn the house down. On one occasion, shots had been fired through the dining room, narrowly missing the incumbent who had been knocking back after-dinner brandies with a guest.

It was an imposing building, its front almost covered in ivy, guarded by a profusion of rhododendrons and exotic trees. To one side, an enormous weeping willow occupied pride of place. It always reminded me of a giant bird - an albatross? - flapping its wings ineffectually, as if it wanted to soar into the blue yonder and was amazed to discover itself firmly rooted in the soil.

Now, there was a lot of activity inside; pointing, painting, slating. To the rear a bulldozer was flattening the rock-garden that had been the Englishman's pride and joy.

'Is the owner about?' I asked a pimply youth who was tending a cement mixer.

'Naw mate. 'E won't be 'ere for a few weeks. Not till it's finished like'.

His accent was pure East End. How long would Bannaher remain popular if he kept importing his workers? Not too long I hoped.

It was several weeks before I saw it again. This time I had Jennifer with me, having finally talked her into spending a day with me.. No workers were visible now; all traces of the recent building activity had vanished. The house looked brighter, more alive somehow, although what brought about this transformation wasn't immediately discernible. Perhaps it was the expanse of pristine gravel driveway at the rear with its high kerbstone edging that now replaced the rock garden, where a gleaming Mercedes stood in the centre.

Jennifer climbed down from behind me and stretched herself. 'So this is the land of your forebears?'

Before I could reply, I heard a voice coming from the clump of rhododendrons to my right.

'This is private property'.

It was clearly Tessa's voice. She emerged from the bushes and I felt myself staring stupidly at her. She had always been striking-looking; now she seemed to have added another dimension. Her eyes looked clearer, her skin smoother, her hair had a softness and bounce that caused it to ripple in the sunlight. And there was a serenity about her that couldn't be totally accounted for by the heavy gold jewelery adorning her neck and wrists, or by the elegant trouser suit that hung so becomingly on her.

She ignored me, focusing entirely on Jennifer, and I realised she hadn't recognised me because of my headgear. I revved up the Triumph then moved it back from the driveway, the exhaust fumes catching on the wind and swirling towards her. She stepped back, her hand flapping, and Jennifer seized the moment to climb back behind me. We sprayed gravel in every direction, and I saw her mouth something, but whatever the message was it got swallowed up by the noise.

We headed up into the foothills behind Croagh, swaying to the rhythm of the bike, swinging this way and that, Jennifer's knees gripping and guiding as we followed the snaking path up the inclines. I could feel the pressure of her breasts against my back and her thighs against my hips as we climbed. What sweet music it turned out to be; idling along the empty road, climbing steadily higher, thunder in my ears, pounding in my chest. And a stalk in my trousers that diamond-drillers would kill for.

The road became narrower, less used, until it was nothing more than a couple of parallel tracks. A watery sun loitered overhead, sometimes completely obscured by the dense patches of forest. Underfoot, a carpet of pine needles deadened the sound of the bike.

Eventually, we emerged from the foothills, and halfway up the mountain the track petered out. We climbed off and I rested my machine against a ditch.

A series of valleys were laid out beneath us; Croagh itself was a collection of matchbox toys, the church spire the only recognisable landmark. We were surrounded by large tracts of forestry land, the dark green of the massed trees broken up here and there by little squares and rectangles of lighter green. Here, ant-like creatures moved about. Cattle or sheep, I supposed. In the distance I could see the hazy outline of the sea. It was as if someone had painted it on the landscape as an afterthought. Shading my eyes, I fancied I saw a boat trawling slowly towards an unknown destination. From up here, it appeared to be traversing the edge of the world; soon it would rise up into the blue sky or drop over the edge. When I looked again it had vanished.

There was a path of sorts on the other side of the stile that barred our progress on the bike. It was overgrown with blackthorn and furze, and could only be negotiated in single file.

'Where does this lead to?', Jennifer asked.

'To another valley.'

'Let's have a look', she said, setting off.

The path wound its way around the contours of the hill, often doubling back on itself, so that the feeling was of going round in circles. Eventually it led to the valley, remote from all its neighbours. Nestling in the bowl were the remains of several homesteads, their derelict condition a monument to the passing of time and people. A deathly silence prevailed; no birds, no bees, no children's laughter, no farmyard sounds. All that remained were the death-throes of civilisation.

This was the place where grandfather had made his poteen. I remembered it from the few times I had been here with Fergus. But I couldn't remember whether it had been before or after grandfather died. He had been born here, and it had been a happy, if not exactly thriving, community in his youth. It didn't matter if nobody had much of anything because everyone helped each other. Gradually, however, their economic plight worsened, and the people left one by one. His father, sustained by his poteen-making, was the last to leave, and on the day of their departure they loaded their few possessions on to the pony and cart, and then demolished the dwelling-house, stone by stone, before leaving. The poteen-making facilities weren't touched however, and within a few months grandad was travelling back to the valley to carry on the tradition.

Looking around me now, I found it hard to believe that anyone could ever have survived here. Most of the surrounding area had been planted with trees, large tracts giving off the perfumed fragrance of spruce and fir. Like a troop of foot soldiers, they were marching down the hillside, getting ever closer to the crumbling dwellings. Soon they would be there, and all trace of human habitation would vanish forever.

'Come on', I said to Jennifer. 'I want to show you something'.

I wasn't too sure where the poteen had been made, but I remembered an old stone building close by the stream, overlooking the pile of stones that had once been the house. We followed the stream now, the path still clearly defined despite the encroaching weeds and bushes. The stream dog-legged sharply left at one point to avoid a grove of gnarled ash and chestnut trees and it was here that we found the old stone building. It was smaller than I remembered and the door, surprisingly, was still intact.

Inside, it was dark and damp. I pulled the door right back to let in some light and was amazed to see an array of utensils and containers arranged against one wall. In one corner a copper pipe twisted its way from a raised tank to another vessel which seemed to be some sort of filtration tank. Under the raised tank stood a gas burner.

Jennifer sniffed. 'This place smells like a brewery'.

'It's where grandad made his moonshine'.

'Made?,' She looked at the room, then at me. 'It looks like he still does'.

'He's been dead fifteen years'.

But I saw what she meant. There was no way this place had been derelict all that time. I moved around, touching surfaces, feeling the thickness of the film of dust. A year or two maybe but no more than that.

'Look at this'.

What Jennifer had called to my attention was a square of lighter colouring on the stone floor. It had obviously been repaired sometime in the recent past and someone had written on the concrete before it set. It read' JAFE -FERGUS 1968.

-

Sometime later we were sipping pints of cold Guinness in Ritchie's. Workmen could be heard banging and sawing over our heads, but Ritchie had taken time off from bawling at them to join us.

'Did you know they were making the stuff?' I asked him, having told him of our discovery. It was only now the shock was wearing off. Fergus had many sides to him - but I hadn't considered poteen-making one of them. After the discovery I had wandered back to the Triumph in a bit of a daze, giving Jennifer a sketchy picture of the family history. I wasn't too sure of it myself anymore.

'Not for a long time', Ritchie replied to my question. 'But I had my suspicions. I followed them one time and found out for sure'.

I shook my head. 'But it's such a small place. Everyone knows everyone else's business. How come I didn't?'

'Nobody did. They were very careful. It took me ages to find out. They were always out hunting and shooting together. Or so everyone thought. And they never sold any around here. They had a fella up West who bought it all. Where he got rid of it I don't know, but none of it ever found its way back here. They were pretty annoyed when they found out I knew. Jafe threatened me with his strong-arm stuff, but I told him if he ever tried that again I'd come back and smash everything to bits'. He laughed. 'I didn't give a fuck about their still. He couldn't see it. I thought it was just a big joke'.

'Do you think your father knew?' This was Jennifer.

I shrugged.

'You could always ask him', said Ritchie.

I looked at him to see if he was being sarcastic then shook my head. 'I couldn't'.

'Let's ask Jennifer. What do you think? Put that journalistic brain of yours to work.

She considered for a moment. 'Well...your grandfather spent a lot of time on the Faulkner farm, more than he spent with you - am I right?' I nodded. 'It follows that he would have needed help as he got older. Your father wouldn't help, that's clear. Jafe and Fergus were close friends; they were the obvious ones to turn to'. She paused. 'Yes, I'd say your father knew'.

'But he never said anything'.

'You don't know that. He may have to Fergus. You haven't exactly been close for years'.

I couldn't argue with that. It seemed I had been going round with my eyes closed for most of my life. I turned to Ritchie, wanting to change the subject.

'Have you heard any more of Bannaher's plans?'

He leaned back in his chair, knitting his hands behind his head. 'My dear brother is the one to ask about that. The latest bulletin from Faulkner house is that they have formed some sort of partnership. His brains and the subby's brawn, something like that'.

I'd seen too much of the subby over the years to underestimate him in the brains department.

'Any idea what they're planning?'

'A killing I expect. I hear they're setting up a batching plant to flog ready-mix concrete to anyone who can afford it. The latest in construction technology, according to Jafe'.

'It can't be Bannaher's idea then. His notion of the latest technology would be a bigger shovel'.

Ritchie laughed. 'It will probably make Jafe's fortune. Something he's been trying to do for years'.

'It will also build Bannaher's complex much cheaper'.

'I hadn't thought of that'.

Ritchie had to leave us then and I spent some minutes explaining my connection with Bannaher to Jennifer. It wasn't the full story but it gave a flavour of what he was like.

'And Tessa, where does she come in?'

'I'm not too sure any more. She...we were friends once'.

'Good friends?'

'You could say that'.

'And now?'

I shrugged. 'She married someone else'.

'But not this Bannaher?'

'No, not him'. I was silent for a while, considering the implications of this. The last time I had seen her was in Manchester - was it really two years ago? - and there was no sign of Larry even then. She had almost certainly dumped him by now. But taking up with Bannaher? And where did Chris fit into the picture?

'I might be able to snoop around, find out what is going on', Jennifer cut into my thoughts. I must have looked vague because she nudged my arm. 'It's what I do, remember?'

It was late when we got back to Limerick, but not too late for her to invite me in for a night-cap. One brandy became two, then three. After that the conversation took a decidedly intimate turn. From there it was only a short step to her bed, where we rolled around removing bits of clothing, with as much decorum as several brandies permit.

'What was she like?' she whispered in my ear, after what seemed like several hurricanes later.

'Not a patch on you', I managed, wondering how the hell I was going to make it to work in a few hours time.

## Chapter fourteen

I didn't know what I expected to find at Ross House, didn't even know what I was looking for if it came to that. The past was gone...I couldn't get it back...better get on with the rest of my life. All these thoughts came flooding into my head as I hunched over my bike, the throttle working overtime. I didn't stop until I was spraying gravel at the front entrance to the house. This time the Mercedes had been replaced by a sporty-looking Mini.

'So it was you the other day', Tessa had the door open before I had removed my helmet. 'I'm not much good at faces but I never forget a helmet'.

'Very droll'. She had changed the trouser-suit for a floral print dress that stopped a few inches above her ankles, but her jewelery was still in place.

'You had better come in'.

I couldn't ever remember being in a room as opulent as the one she led me to. The curtains were velvet, the settee leather, the table a rich, dark oak that could seat a dozen at a sitting without any trouble. An enormous dresser stood against one wall, books lining the breakfront bottom, the open top displaying expensive-looking pieces of glass and silverware.

'You've come a long way, Tessa', I said, slowly taking in the room. 'This all your own handiwork?'

'Oh no. The previous owner had good taste if nothing else. My only contribution was re-arranging it'. She studied me. 'You look different'.

'I'm working for a living now'.

'Leopards do change their spots then'.

'Only some of them'.

'Do I detect a touch of sarcasm, Terry?'

I grew tired of the verbal tennis.

'Look, I didn't come here to talk about me...'

'No, I don't expect you did. What **did** you come for?'

I really hadn't a clue now.

'Where's Larry?'

'You came looking for Larry! What makes you think he would be here?'

'He's your husband, isn't he?'

She shrugged. 'We split up ages ago. I thought you would have known. It was over between us a long time ago'.

'I never thought there was anything to be over between you in the first place'. I sneered. 'Apart from the money'.

She didn't reply, but helped herself to a cigarette from an inlaid box. I declined her offer of one.

'You didn't really think he was here, did you?'

I shrugged. 'With you, you can never tell. You might want him as a trophy or something'. I smiled thinly. 'You know, like a stag's head over your fireplace'.

A scowl crossed her face. 'Larry was a fool'.

'Weren't we all? I know I was'.

'No. I mean a real fool. All he wanted to do was play the horses and dogs. Every day. We had a business to run'.

'Ah yes, the business. That has a familiar ring', I paused, expecting her to say something, but she didn't. 'Anyway, you knew what he was like when you married him'.

She shook her head. 'Not what he was really like'.

'Why should you care? All you wanted was the money. Our money. Don't tell me any different'.

She paused in the act of drawing on her cigarette. 'Suppose it were true - just suppose - and I had put the proposition to you instead, what would you have done?'

'You admit it then? You admit you got Larry to steal our money in return for marrying you?'

She smiled. 'It's a hypothetical question, Terry. Just a game. Come on, what would you do with a proposition like that?'

I didn't answer. I couldn't answer. She knew I couldn't answer and began to laugh softly.

'That's no sort of question', I said angrily.

'But it is. It's every sort of question'. She snapped her fingers. 'I might have been that much away from asking you instead of Larry'.

'It **is** true then? '

'Maybe - maybe not'.

This time I got really mad. 'Jesus, can't you answer a simple question? I don't care anymore, I really don't. Just tell me if it's true'. She didn't answer.

'Answer me this then, you bitch. Why didn't you tell me you and Chris were brother and sister?'

This time I did rattle her. Not much, but I heard a slight intake of breath.

'Who told you that?'

'Never mind. It's true though, isn't it?'

She shrugged, at ease again. 'It's no big deal'.

'Isn't it? When we were first introduced Chris pretended had only just met you'.

'That was true. When we were very young, mother split us up. She sent him to live with an aunt in Galway and kept me. When he finally found out, he spent years following my trail, till he eventually caught up with me'.

'I don't understand all the secrecy'.

'It's hard to explain to other people. It was easier to pass me off as a stranger. Which I was in a way'.

'That stuff about your mother and brother Ben...?'

'All made up. Mother died five years ago. That's what made it so hard for Chris to trace me'.

'So what did you...I mean, Manchester, and all those other times you were away...?'

She stubbed the cigarette viciously against the ashtray. 'Oh Christ, can't you see anything? Do I have to spell it out for you?'

'Yes you do, actually'.

'You asked for it'. She gave a thin laugh. 'I was on the game. Where do you think the money to start the business came from in the first place? Those times I was away I was usually with clients. A week in Bournemouth, a month in Manchester, a dirty weekend in Brighton... You name it, I did it'.

'Did Chris know?'

'Did he know? That's a laugh. He arranged most of them'.

This time I couldn't keep the surprise from showing. 'Chris, a ponce!'

'Don't look so shocked. Are you any better?'

'I never put a woman on the game'.

'I was already on it. He knew straight away what I was...'

'I should'a known after Brighton'. I couldn't keep the bitterness from my voice.

'You got your money's-worth. Don't tell me you didn't. You were just another rung on the ladder...'

'Is that all it was...?

She laughed. 'Love...or something like that? Oh, come on!'

'I didn't mean...love. But didn't you even...like me? I thought we had...something'.

'Sure. We had a good time. Didn't we?'

'Yeah. We had a good time'.

109

'That's something. Don't expect too much and you'll never be disappointed, that's what my mother always said'. She paused a moment. 'I was only doing it until I had enough to get out, but Chris saw straight away that I wasn't going to make it, not with the sort of punters I was getting. 'Corporate Punters', that's what he came up with; organised orgies for businessmen with plenty of lolly'.

'But your own brother...?'

'Grow up, Terry. What does it matter what our relationship was? It was a business thing, nothing more. We were both determined to get out from under the shit-heap. This was merely one more avenue'.

'Is that all Larry and I were... tickets to ride?'

'You could have been part of it, remember? I offered it to you'.

I didn't reply.

'I saw what poverty did to my mother. She moved from one dingy flat to another, always one step in front of the debt collectors, trailing her current boyfriend with her. Those that didn't beat her up bled her dry. I left when I was sixteen and swore that I would never go back to that sort of life. Never'.

'None of our lives are perfect'.

'Most people's lives are shit. They're desperate. And most of them don't do anything about it. Well fuck that...', she waved a hand. 'Getting this far took a lot of doing. Getting the rest of the way should be easier'.

'There's more?'

'Of course there's more. We have plans that would blow your mind'.

'We...?'

''Pat'.

'Pat?' I had to think for a moment. 'Well now, isn't that cosy?' I couldn't resist a dig. 'He's old enough to be your father'.

'Not quite. Maybe you see him as a father figure, but I don't. I think he's cuddly'.

Bannaher cuddly! I couldn't stop laughing.

'He's about as cuddly as an orangutan. Still, it's your funeral...'

'This is a new beginning for both of us. We both sold everything we had in England to make a fresh start here'.

'You make it sound like a marriage'.

'It will be. As soon as my divorce comes through'.

I couldn't say I was too surprised.

'And Larry, what does he have to say?'

'He's going along with it. It's in his interest...his financial interest'.

'He's been bought off you mean'. I laughed. 'Then, Larry was always buyable, wasn't he?' I looked at the large ormolu clock on the sideboard. Fifteen minutes, that was all I had been here. It felt like a week. 'I must admit you had me fooled completely. Never once did it cross my mind that you had been selling yourself...' I smiled...'and not so cheaply at that. But then, it's not the sort of behaviour you expect from your business partner, is it? Tell me, that night in Manchester,was that one of your orgies? You, Bannaher, and...?' I let my voice trail away.

'Don't be silly. That was a legitimate business meeting'.

'But Pat was part of the grand plan...?

'Of course not. That was all behind me by then'.

'But he approves?' She was silent. 'He doesn't approve?'

'He doesn't know'.

'Now, there's a good start to a relationship. What if he finds out?'

'Who's going to tell him?'

'I might'.

'He wouldn't believe you'.

'No, probably not. But it would be embarrassing, wouldn't it?'

'What do you want, Terry?' Have you come here to blackmail me?'

'How could I? I didn't know till now'.

'So what do you want?'

I shook my head. 'I don't know. I really don't know. I thought maybe...'

'You want to fuck me, don't you?' She must have seen something in my eyes. 'You really do, don't you?' She laughed. 'Well why not? It's not as if you're a stranger. And we did have some good times...' She moved close to me and I could feel her hand on my crotch. 'My, my, you are pleased to see me...'

A mixture of excitement and self-loathing filled me. I could...I could really make love to her and no one would ever know. I wanted to, Jesus I wanted to. She wanted me to, didn't she? She was laughing as she undid my fly. I pushed her away roughly.

'I can't afford you, Tessa. I never could'. I hurried to the door. 'You stick with Pat. You were made for each other'.

I was several miles down the road before I realised I had forgotten to ask her about Chris.

-

'Fill 'er up', Moynihan instructed Jango' handing him the hip-flask. 'Those Clare winds have a way of sneaking up on a body'.

111

Five minutes later we were all piling into Jango's station wagon, and shortly after that we were hitting the potholes on the Ennis road with great accuracy.

'Fucking gophers', observed Moynihan. 'All we need now is the rain'.

By the time we passed through Lisdoonvarna the rain was sweeping inland, a great sheet of it racing across The Burren. We didn't stop but continued on to Doolin, hoping to see the Arran Islands off-shore.

'Those wet rocks in the Atlantic, that's what Synge called them', Moynihan informed us. 'Did any of ye ever see The Playboy of The Western World? Now there was a play and a half'.

I laughed. 'Christy Mahon, the last playboy of the western world. He'd have made a good subby...' Moynihan looked at me...'thick as a couple of four be two's nailed together'.

The village of Doolin lay sunken below the coastal shelf, and looked in imminent danger of being swamped by the tidal onslaught battering the jagged rocks surrounding it.

'Turn back', shouted Moynihan, as we stared at the grey blanket obscuring everything in sight.

'We'd have more chance of seeing Moby Dick'.

As we passed back through Lisdoonvarna, I noticed that the pubs were open.

'Anyone fancy a pint?'

Lisdoon; all narrow streets and tall hotels. Where old farmers came looking for young wives. Or maybe just to get their leg over. Not this wet Sunday morning though; just desultory little gatherings at fogged-up windows, slowly sipping black pints, watching the rain scudding by.

The hotel we choose looked as if it had been badly frightened many years ago. Green-painted windows and sills, the paint peeling or absent from the wooden frames, the once-grey walls lined with cracks zigzagging from eaves to windows. Inside, everywhere was paneled; dark brown below eye-level, honey-coloured elsewhere. The ceiling owed its rich hue to the effects of nicotine. We were the only customers apart from the golden retriever steaming by the fire.

Jango and Moyhihan joined the dog, leaving Jennifer and myself to listen to the barman. Before long he was telling us his life story, and bemoaning the lack of what he called 'social pastimes' in the modern world.

'The crack, all gone', he moaned. 'Look at it, a ghost town. We might as well shut up, 'cept for the few months of the summer. I remember the time when you couldn't walk down the street for women...'

'Women? I thought it was the other way round'.

He shook his head. 'Don't you believe it. The women here were at it long before the men. Why, when I first started here in the fifties, the hotel held dances every night for the guests. Fightin' for the privilege we were. And most of them were women. Young and old. Lookin' for a man...any sort of man'. I could see Jennifer giving him a skeptical look. 'It's true enough. Fellas were in scarce supply in them days, emigration you know. I was sent out around the town to round up any spare ones floatin' about. We'd bribe them with offers of free drinks. Sometimes when things got really bad, we'd pile the women into the back of the old van and take them to a dance where we knew there was a supply of men'.

'You make it sound like some sort of service-centre for frustrated females'.

He began polishing the already-gleaming counter. 'I didn't mean to imply that miss. I'm sure a lot of it was innocent fun'. He finished polishing. 'And sure if it wasn't, what harm? Isn't that what makes the world go round'.

'I think he was making it up', she said later in the car.

'Well now', said Jango, mellowed by the addition of several whiskies to his system. 'I'm not so sure I like the idea of being chased by women. I mean...it would take all the excitement away...'

''There wouldn't be too many chasing an ugly ould fucker like you'. Moynihan said, a big grin on his face. 'Not unless they were coffin-dodgers themselves'.

By now the weather had cleared up and we were headed for the point-to-point meeting at Neville's Farm, the event that had brought us out in the first place.

Neville's Farm was the ideal venue for a race meeting; big open fields with a fine covering of grass, long galloping sections where a horse could stretch, and a mixture of natural obstacles and man-made fences.

'Didn't you fancy a bet?' Jennifer asked after her first-race fancy had ploughed into the stone wall that was the third obstacle. The jockey shot over the wall and slid along the grass on the other side, into a dark blob of cowshit. He picked himself up, cursing loudly, and went to retrieve his mount, which was struggling to its feet on the take-off side.' Useless cunt', I heard someone shout.

Of course I fancied a bet. Just as much as the drug addict fancies the next fix or the wino the next bottle. But I had been down that road. I wasn't planning to come back up it just yet.

I left them to it. The ruins of an old castle sat on a hill directly behind, so I climbed up to it. It was nothing much; just a collection of broken-down walls with mounds of earth ramped up to make it safe. A stream meandered around the base, eventually crossing the racecourse, where it was incorporated into one of the fences. I found a spot that sheltered me from the wind and squatted there, smoking. I watched the next couple of races that way.

Jennifer joined me after a while and we amused ourselves trying to hit a tin can that had caught on a twig by the edge of the stream.

'Rivers become crooked by taking the path of least resistance', she said. 'I read that somewhere'.

'Sounds like my bloody epitaph', I replied, flinging a whole handful of stones and dislodging the can.

'Was it really bad?' she asked after I had given her an edited version of my gambling habits.

'My London period - I'm calling it that now - was great at the time. Looking back, I see it differently. I was like a junkie needing a fix...I had to have that bet. Even if it was only two flies climbing up a wall, I had to have it. And I was willing to do almost anything to get it. I suppose I should regret it, but you can't just wipe it away...'

'It's sad when friends fall out. You were very close, weren't you? You, Larry, Bannaher...'

'Bannaher was never my friend. He was just there. You couldn't walk down the streets of Kilburn or Cricklewood without seeing some evidence of his existence. At six every morning, the green Transit vans filled to the brim with hung-over navvies heading off to the building sites to shovel shit for the day. At six in the evening, the same gangs trudging into the pubs to spend the day's sub. At closing time, staggering back to a stinking room in a run-down house, or, worse still, to kip in an all-night launderette or in the doorway of Burtons or John Colliers. That was Bannaher's world, or at least the world of them misfortunate enough to work for him. Oh I know, there are those who will say if it wasn't him it would be someone else. And that's true. There would be someone else. There always is. But to make out that he's some kind of public benefactor? 'A great man', was how I once heard someone describe him, 'sure isn't he providing work for half the county?' Jaysus, all he's doing is getting rich trading in human misery'.

'Listen, Terry...'

'We hated his guts. Larry most of all. Chris wouldn't work for him. None of us would'. I laughed. 'We weren't prejudiced mind, in those days we wouldn't work for anyone. And look at us now'. I stood up and brushed some dirt from my trousers. 'It's just that I thought I was far away from that bastard. Come on, I'll buy you a cup of tea'.

A large red-headed man was slurping tea noisily at the tea-wagon when I called my order. It was Costello, Fergus's old boss.

'You're Terry', he said, as soon as he set eyes on me.

I nodded, excused myself for a moment to take Jennifer her tea, then returned. We chatted idly for a while; he had a horse running in one race, which was his main reason for being here, then I turned the conversation to what I really wanted to talk about.

'You knew Fergus was making the poteen, I suppose?'

He looked at me for a long time then nodded slowly. 'I used some on the animals as a liniment. Good for rheumy joints'.

'You didn't drink it then?'

He laughed. 'Jaysus that stuff would kill you'.

'You knew that Jafe was in on it too?'

'You thinking of starting up again?' He snorted. 'Stay away from Jafe is my advice. Anyway he wouldn't be interested now. He's got bigger fish to fry'.

'Why should I stay away from him?'

''I meant keep your money away from him. He tends to be a bit absent-minded when it comes to paying it back. The farm barely paid for itself until recently. Over the years I'd say it's the poteen that's kept him afloat, then a few years ago he discovered the sand-pit and it proved to be a life-saver. However, he needed capital to start up, and I staked him to some of it. Foolishly, as it turned out'.

'He never paid you back? But he looks to be cleaning up now'.

'That's Jafe for you'.

'You said some of the money...'

'Fergus put some in too. Other's as well for all I know...'

'He didn't get paid either?'

'Not that I know of. He had mentioned it to me some weeks before the accident. He wanted the money for something and Jafe was pleading poverty as usual'.

'They fell out...?'

'No, not that. But he wasn't very happy. Then came the accident. Jafe was very cut up, being the driver and all. I didn't think the time was right to ask about my investment...'

'I never knew Jafe was the driver'.

He nodded. 'I remember Fergus telling me that they were making a delivery that evening. Just as well the accident happened on the way back. There would have been hell to pay otherwise. All that stuff in the boot...'

'There was hell to pay anyway...'

'I'm sorry. I didn't mean...'

'That's okay. It was definitely an accident, I suppose...?'

'Yes, of course. What are you thinking?'

I finished my tea and threw the cup in the bin. 'I'm not thinking anything. I just wondered is all'.

# Chapter fifteen

Jimmy, Tom Whyte's assistant, put us temporarily out of work by falling into one of the trenches and breaking his leg. Some union representatives inspected the site shortly afterwards and declared themselves unhappy with site safety. Representations were made to the company but nothing came of it. The following day pickets were placed at several locations, and Tom Whyte was one of the most vociferous in urging a complete stop to the work until pay and conditions had been improved.

Little groups congregated outside the picket lines, discussing and arguing, watching other groups doing the same thing. And all waiting to see who would be first to cross the picket lines. They milled around, most of them wanting to go to work, nearly all agreeing that it wasn't inadequate safety that had caused Jimmy's accident, but himself. *'Sure isn't he a bit simple anyway; a building site's no place for the likes of him'* . Yet no one wanted to make the first move. I immersed myself in the middle of one such group.

When it became apparent that no one was going to break ranks we began to drift away, some to the outlying farms and smallholdings where they had other tasks to occupy them, others to their rooms in the city to sleep or watch TV. More of us adjourned to the pubs, where, tongues loosened, we catalogued all the iniquities and injustices that were the lot of the working man. By late afternoon most of us were roaring drunk, pledging unceasing solidarity to the struggle against…well, whatever the fight was about. By evening we were trying to sleep it off, hoping that the morning would be both hang-over and picket-free.

In reality, nothing had changed. The pickets were still there, Tom Whyte was shouting louder than before, and the murmuring groups were still as indecisive as ever.

Shortly before starting time, a Blue Transit wove its way through the idling groups and pulled up near where I was standing. Moynihan was driving. The side door slid open and I could see several welders and riggers seated inside.

'Get in', Moynihan shouted.

I stood there, indecisive, feeling embarrassed.

'Get in', he shouted again. 'You're employed as a welder - and that's what you're going to do today'.

'You'll find no strike-breakers here', Whyte and several others moved in front of me, preventing me from entering the van even if I had wanted to. 'Take your scabs back to where they came from'.

'Yeah, the arsehole of England', someone shouted behind me.

I couldn't hear Moyhinan's reply, but his face looked the perfect setting for a gathering storm. The side door slammed shut, the wheels spat gravel, then the van shot past us.

''They might be in', Whyte said quietly in its wake, 'but they still have to come back out'.

That night in the Cavern, Whyte was in a buoyant mood.

'Fill 'em up', he told Jango. 'We showed them what was what, eh? This is one battle we're going to win hands down'.

'Aye, but who is winning the war? Who's winning that?' Jango placed our two pints on the counter.

'War? There is no war. We scuttled them good and proper today. Their Transit is upside down in the canal. They won't be back tomorrow. No siree!'

Jango wiped the counter dry. 'It's always been a war. It was when the Tolpuddle martyrs tried to form a trade union, and were sentenced to seven long years in Van Diemen's Land for their troubles. It was when Churchill called out the army to the striking miners in 1926. It was when British officers forced British soldiers out of the trenches at gunpoint in the Somme. It's the class war, see?'

'Class war? This is fuck-all do with class'

'You sure about that? When you aspire to better your lot, what are you doing? Social climbing, that's what. Better job, bigger car, bigger house, then becoming the boss yourself...what's that all about if it's not about class?' As he moved away to serve somebody else he began to sing;

'Oh the working class can kiss my arse

I've got the foreman's job at last'

He returned a few minutes later. 'Don't get me wrong, I'm not knocking you boys. But it's always been like that. Dog eat dog...except that the ruling classes usually have the bigger dogs'.

'We have right on our side'.

'You sure about that?' Jango looked steadily at Whyte for what seemed an age before speaking again. 'Look, don't assume that just because they are on the other side you're dealing with a bunch of idiots. Walls have ears...especially pub walls. If I can hear things so will others'.

'What was that about?' I asked when we were alone again.

'Well, you might as well know, I suppose'. He looked over to the far end of the bar where Jango was now serving. 'Jimmy shouldn't have been on the site at all because he's epileptic. That's why he broke his leg; he had a fit and fell in'.

'Jesus! That's great, that is'.

'It won't be too bad if we can keep it quiet...'

I looked at him. 'In this town? No fucking chance. The dogs'll be barking it from the Markets Field before the night is out'.

'Look, Jimmy had the same right to make a living as the rest of us. He's fine as long as he remembers to take his tablets. He forgets sometimes is all'. He shrugged. 'Besides, he's my sister's boy. I promised her I'd look after him'.

*And a fine job you've done of it, and he lying in the Regional with a broken leg.* I didn't know too much about epilepsy but I had the feeling that a building site was the last place an epileptic should be.

The day had dragged interminably. The morning was aimless, though livened up by the rage of some of the strikers at the welding they could see going on in the distance. Most of us had resisted the lure of the pub during the day because there was now a realisation that the trouble might not, after all, be resolved too quickly. If that was the case then we had better pace ourselves.

At lunchtime I had met Jennifer for coffee and sticky buns in a tiny side-street café that baked all its own bread. Jennifer had been assigned to cover the strike and spent most of the time trying to pick my brains.

''You're not a bit interested in me', I said, 'only in what you can find out.

'Come on Terry, she pleaded. 'I have a deadline. What's going on? Will ye be back to work tomorrow?'

'Your guess is as good as mine. We may find out at the meeting'.

The meeting was held in the Mechanics Institute, a public building that hired out room for meetings and other social diversions. That afternoon had seen about forty of us congregate there, first to hear a union official tell us that as the strike was unofficial the company was within their rights not to talk to us. This it was so doing, and unless we went back to work there would be no talks. He was howled down; the crossing of the picket lines that morning had put a different complexion on things.

Then Tom Whyte stood up and had his say.

'The Irish workers are the blacks of Europe. Slaves in our own country. This company...' he snapped his fingers...'couldn't care that much about our welfare. An English company, mind you, not an Irish one'. He paused. 'An

English company that is at this moment working away with its scabs and blacklegs'.

'They won't get very far without somebody to dig their trenches for them', someone shouted.

'What's to stop them bringing in more scab labour?'

'Over our dead bodies', the crowd roared

In the end, it was decided that nothing, nobody, would pass the picket lines from now on. And if physical force were needed, there were enough of us to overturn any car or van that tried to get through.

We hadn't waited for the morning however; someone had seen the Transit leave the site after work and had noted where it had been parked. As soon as it was dark, four of us had bounced it into the nearby canal, which was why Whyte now wore a pleased look on his face. How long the van would remain there was anyone guess; the canal was tidal and by morning it could be half way to America.

Moynihan was waiting for me when I got back to my room after closing time. Where he had concealed himself I don't know, but as I shoved the key in the lock he was by my side, pushing me inside.

'Quick, I don't want anyone to see me!'

Inside, there was hardly room to draw breath; the bed, a recessed area with a curtained front for storing clothes, and a leather armchair with squeaky cushions. A yellow lampshade swung imperceptibly overhead, creating a slight movement of light on the far wall. I threw myself down on the bed.

'I can understand why you wouldn't pass the pickets today', Moynihan said. 'Nobody wants to be branded a strike-breaker. Tomorrow we'll do things differently. The van will pick you up from here. Okay?'

They obviously hadn't heard of its fate yet.

'What makes you think I want to be picked up?'

'You're the only one on strike employed directly by the company. The others are all working for a sub-contractor'. He laughed, 'They'll be out of a job after tomorrow - there's plenty more willing to take their places'. He shrugged. 'It's up to you'.

'If I don't go with you I'm out of a job too, is that it?'

'It's not up to me'.

'I'll take my chances'.

In the morning there was pandemonium on site. Whyte, true to his promise, intended it would be easier to get into Mountjoy jail than to get past our picket lines. A solid wall, three deep, barred the way. An unfamiliar yellow van drew up, and this time the site manager got out.

'Let us through. You're preventing people from going about their legitimate work. 'Stand back there'. He waved to Moynihan who was behind the wheel. 'Come on, come through'.

The van inched forward, but it was forced to stop when it was surrounded by angry picketers. It was either stop or drive over us.

'Stand firm lads. Stand firm'. Whyte could be heard shouting.

Then the van began to rock. I was trapped in the centre of the growling, truculent gathering, convinced by now that we had been wrongly treated. I leant my weight to the body-power that was making the van bounce alarmingly.

'Fuck this for a game', I heard Moynihan shout. Then he climbed out and walked, unhindered, through the mob.

The crew in the back of the van tried to do the same but weren't so lucky. Kicks, punches and spits rained down on them as they ran the gauntlet of angry faces. They were forced to retreat, several of them with bloodied faces, jeering and cheering following them as they headed back the way they had come.

An hour later they were back, this time with a Garda escort. The booing and jeering resumed as they were allowed, albeit reluctantly, to pass. Whyte winked at me as the van bumped along the path to the work area. For a while the air was filled with the noise of plant and machinery starting up. Then, gradually, each machine stuttered and fell silent.

'It's always wise to have a few strings to your bow' Whyte quipped, clapping me on the back. 'Come on, let's get some breakfast'.

Every morning afterwards a police presence was required to escort the handful of workers still braving it out. Some had already cried enough and bailed out as soon as the trouble erupted, and each new day brought loud cheers as the size of the group dwindled.

The skirmishing and sabotage continued; not so much the machinery anymore because it now had security guards keeping an eye on it, but there were other, unguarded stretches that were easy targets. Sections of pipe, already in position and waiting to be welded, were ripped out, trenches were filled in, one section completely flooded by damming a stream and diverting it. The Gardai drove around making cursory checks, but it didn't seem as if their hearts were in it.

By now the media had got hold of the story and reporters from the national newspapers were sniffing around, looking for unusual slants on the dispute.

121

Inevitably, the TV crews turned up, and one evening saw us watching ourselves in a news item on RTE. Tom Whyte, flanked by myself and several others, filled the screen while a reporter prattled away.

'...initially, this was a dispute about safety but it has now escalated into a row about pay and conditions and - more importantly - the use of foreign labour on site. On one side the striking locals, on the other a highly paid team of welders and steel workers imported from England...'

The picture focussed on Whyte... 'Union shop-steward Tom Whyte refused to be interviewed, but told me earlier... 'we are working in the same conditions for a fraction of the pay of these so-called skilled men. Why couldn't all the workers be recruited locally? There are many good tradesmen sitting on their backsides, watching their work being done by scabs from John Bull'...' The item ended with the site manager saying that the company would never bow to threats and intimidation, and that the movement of labour been the two countries had never been an issue. For many years thousands of Irish workers had been crossing the Channel to find work, why weren't a handful of British workers free to do the same?

The following day two badly beaten welders forced him to change his mind. Everybody was laid off and the site closed until further notice.

For several more days we turned up at the site, idling the time away, waiting to see what new tactics the company might try. After a while it dawned on us that they weren't planning anything - least not in the immediate future. The hired plant and machinery was removed from site, everything else battened down or locked away, and Moyhihan was dispatched to a job in Scotland. I spoke to him briefly before he left and learned that he expected to be away for several weeks. He didn't seem too upset; 'I hope I never again set eyes on this city of knackers and wandering horses'.

It looked like we were in for a long siege so we drew up a rota for picket duty. A token presence was all that was now required, leaving the rest of us free to do as we pleased.

'I don't know why you bother', Jennifer said one evening. 'Seeing as you are all out of jobs now'.

This was true; all of us had received dismissal notices, citing gross industrial misconduct as the main reason.

'A load of bullshit', said Whyte. 'The company has to talk to the unions if it wants the site re-opened. We'll get our jobs back'.

Jennifer had news for me too. Her enquiries about Bannaher in London had brought news about a hurried departure.

'It was the tax man. Too close for comfort was how my contact put it. A demand for a hundred thousand pounds. He bought time by paying off some of it, then sold all his assets and made a quick getaway. I believe there's a warrant out over there for him'.

'Somebody should tell them where he is'.

'They know where he is. They can't do anything about it. Not for a tax bill. So long as he stays put he's safe'.

'The bloody bogman is laughing at them again'.

I made several trips back to Croagh, ostensibly to see mother and father, but I was also curious to see what Bannaher was up to. Ritchie, as usual, had his finger on the pulse.

'Blasting', he informed me. 'They intend blasting the Hill. And crushing the rock to make concrete'.

Indeed, the process had already begun. I saw buildings taking shape in the distance, and a long conveyor-type structure under construction. A bulldozer was beavering away at the base of the hill.

I remembered the last time we had hunted rabbits around its environs. Ritchie , myself and Hopper McGrath. Ritchie had rigged up a spotlight, which he carried on his back in an old school satchel, whilst Hopper and myself trudged in his wake. A black, moonless night speared occasionally by a shaft of light from Ritchie's contraption. Sometimes revealing a rabbit, sitting there, dazzled.

It was a pastime we indulged regularly in on long winter nights. Apart from the pleasure we derived, there was also a few bob to be made selling the skins. That night we merely went through the motions; switching the light off and letting the rabbits escape. We had worked our way back towards the river then sat by a clump of rocks known as Poll Dubh. Poll Dubh, Black Hole. By now the moon had come out and the moonbeams striking the water created pools of shimmering light, but Poll Dubh, hidden by tall rocks and clumps of bushes, was a dark, shadowy mass.

'It won't be the same when you're gone', said Hopper.

'It's not forever. I'll be back''

'No more dazzling though'.

I shrugged. 'Who knows'.

Ritchie, silent during this exchange, suddenly grabbed the satchel and hurried away. Soberly, we followed, remembering that his father had drowned on the same spot some ten or twelve years back.

I looked at the Hill now, and at the ants beavering away at its base. Would it still be there in twenty five years time? Or would it be flattened like everything else that came into contact with Bannaher? I shook my head; it wasn't a hill, it was a fucking mountain. It would still be there when the likes of Bannaher were long gone.

## Chapter sixteen

The new of my father's death was conveyed to me in the middle of the night. I woke to it gradually, the alcoholic fog on my brain reluctant to clear at first. When I saw the Garda outside my door it didn't sink in at all. The only thing that registered was the words *'bad news'*, and I found myself thinking *'surely this could wait till morning'*. It was only when the word *'dead'* finally penetrated that reality surfaced.

'Dead?' I looked at him, stupidly. 'Who is dead?'

I could see him shake his head then turn away from the noxious fumes wafting his way. 'I've been trying to tell you. Your father. Your local Garda station contacted us and asked us to let you know. I am sorry to be the bearer of such bad news...'

I found myself nodding. Inside I felt empty. He could have been telling me my tax disc had expired for all the impact it made. At least my frantic urge of a few moments ago to spew up all over the corridor had receded, although my mouth felt as if I had swallowed a pint of creosote.

'My mother...how is she?'

'I have no information on that. It was your parish priest, Fr Maguire who contacted our colleagues. If you get in touch with him...'

Then he was gone into the night, leaving me staring stupidly in his wake, wondering what sort of police force it was that went round in the middle of the night telling people their father was dead.

Sobering up in the shower took about half an hour and three black coffees. I sat for a while contemplating what to do, then wrote a note and shoved it under my next-door neighbours door. Shortly afterwards I climbed aboard the Triumph, feeling like I had gone a couple of rounds with Mohammed Ali.

By the time I reached our boreen the sun was clambering over the horizon - an orange ball so bright it hurt my eyes. I couldn't recall seeing a sunrise before, certainly not in recent years, and certainly not one as beautiful as this. The sudden appearance of the sun over the sea, glinting on the water, changing the colour of everything, held me spellbound. It was as if the covers were being peeled back and the true complexion of the world laid bare before my eyes.

My appearance in the boreen frightened a choir of birds. Larks I guess, who had been regaling each other from the blackthorn bushes that surrounded the house. They dispersed noisily. A couple of cats emerged from the privet hedges and regarded me with suspicion before disappearing again. When I was young, I had crawled as competently as any cat amongst those same hedges.

The house was silent and locked up, the curtains drawn, no whiff of life emanating from the interior. I found the spare key under the rainwater barrel and let myself in.

Mother wasn't home, that was for sure. The bedroom she and father had shared all those years looked back with foreboding as I gazed through its half-open door. The bed had been stripped of its contents. It reminded me of a skeleton; an iron frame with flaky brass-plated knobs adorning the bed-ends, and wooden boards set between angle-iron runners. The mattress had been tipped up and lay at an angle, wedged between the frame and the wall. The bed-ends were similar to many I had seen blocking gaps in roadside fields up and down the country.

A wave of sadness overcame me as I realised this dingy little room, with its flimsy wardrobe, it's tiny chest of drawers and its picture of Pope Pious on the wall, was all my mother now had left. Fergus gone; now my dad gone too. There was me, but I hadn't counted for a long time. As I shut the door I noticed the candlestick that had lighted father's way to bed in the days before electricity. A new candle stood in the holder.

Back in the kitchen I looked at my watch. Too early to call on Fr Maguire and find out where my mother was. I put the kettle on and looked around. Apart from the kitchen, there were only three more rooms, the bedroom I had just come from, the one shared by Fergus and myself, and the scullery, which had been converted into a washroom and toilet.

I couldn't resist a peek in my old bedroom, although I knew well enough what I would find. Fergus's bed made up, all his clothes still inside the built-in cupboard, the bookcase and dressing-table still crammed with his books and other possessions. The framed pictures of him, some showing him aboard Costello's nags, and a grainy blown-up one of him aboard his Triumph. Of me there was no trace.

Back in the kitchen, I sat in father's chair, the one he had carved himself, and lit a cigarette. It didn't surprise me that it wasn't very comfortable. It was too upright, made you sit up straight, and was hard on the backside. The seat was a solid wooden panel, the only concession to comfort a cushion filled with chaff. I realised now that everything about my father was hard; the chair, his bed, even the bread he ate. He ate only stale bread - it had to be at least two days old - and he sliced it as if cutting wood with a handsaw.

Sitting there, feeling the chair's roughness, seeing the photo of Fergus and myself on the mantelpiece, him curly-haired and laughing, me with my hair centre-parted and squirming in his lap, I felt like closing my eyes and staying that way for ever. There were other photos on the shelf, including one of father and mother, taken on a beach somewhere, on their wedding day. I could see the date etched on the right-hand corner; 26th March 1939. Father was wearing his hat at a jaunty angle, a huge grin lighting up his face. I had forgotten what a handsome man he'd been...

Memories came flooding back; the stony fields...the Hill rising steeply at the back...seeing him again, picking up stones and casting them towards the ditch...showing me how to open drills and sow potatoes...learning how to set cabbages plants using string line. The animals that were part of my childhood moving again amongst the rocks and bushes...the sow and her litter of banbhs, the squeals of the young males as he took a razor blade to them, their little balls popping out on the floor. The sheep-shearing, a summer ritual that went on for weeks, shearing one or two animals each evening after work. I could see clearly the chase to capture the sheep, father stood over it with its head trapped between his thighs, while I held on to its back legs. He clipped the sheep slowly with a machine he had bought by post, and when he was finished there were dozens of nicks on the misfortunate animal's neck. As each barbered sheep galloped away, I marveled at how unlike their coated brothers they looked. Not like sheep at all in fact, more like plucked geese. At the end of the operation the machine was stowed carefully away in its original box and put aside for another year.

He was a very methodical man, I realised. A place for everything, and everything in its place. Thursday night was shaving night, a ritual that never changed. The little table he used was still in place in the corner of the kitchen. I could still see it now, laid out like an operating table by mother. Boiling water in the chipped enamel basin, jug of cold water beside it, his razor and new Macs Smile blade all neatly laid out. Whisking up enough lather to cover his face always seemed to take an age, and when he was finished all you could see were his eyeballs peering out from the white forest. Sometimes he managed to get soap in his eyes, then he danced around the kitchen shouting '*the towel, where's the fecking towel!*'

He didn't believe in barbers, so had purchased a hair-clipping machine from the same source that supplied the shears, and as I got older he showed me how to use it on his hair. He had several lumps on his head the size of gooseberries, and I was afraid at first that I would slice them off and his brains would fall out. I could see the clippers now, still in its box, sitting on the ledge over the fireplace. A film of dust had gathered on top of it. I finished my cigarette and stood up. His brains hadn't fallen out, his heart had exploded instead.

That evening, in the little mortuary attached to the hospital, I couldn't look at him. He lay there in his box, waxen face staring into infinity, looking much better in death than he ever had in life...*and I couldn't look at him.* I knelt at the back of the room, surrounded by mourners, and only when the lid was being screwed down did I look in his direction.

People were falling over themselves to be kind, I found. Death drew them closer together, brought out the best in people. The departed ones were merely going on a journey; '*sure isn't it a better place he's going to*'. I couldn't accept this easy acquaintance with death; but then, if I had found it difficult to come to terms with my father when he was alive, what chance was there now that he was dead? Death ended all negotiations; all the things left unsaid would never be said now.

The cortege departed the city slowly, and wend its way through the early summer evening, where a brief shower had washed the countryside clean and left it sparkling beneath a burst of last-minute sunshine. The convoy took the long road to the village church - no hurry now, was there? - slowing to a crawl as it passed our house. The path to the church was lined with people, all blessing themselves as we crawled by, the men-folk respectfully removing their caps. I saw real sorrow on the faces; real tears even. Here was one of their own taken from them, a man who had walked amongst them for almost seventy years. Fought with them, worked with them, lived amongst them, and now had died amongst them. And they were now paying their respects. It made me feel like an intruder.

The following morning the sky was leaden and the fields muddy, and the Atlantic Ocean was howling in the bay a few miles away. The seagulls were screeching a bizarre funeral rite as we followed the coffin to its final haven.

My mother stood glassy-eyed between her cousin and myself, the small graveyard unable to support all the mourners, and they had spilled out into the roadside in their dozens. They huddled together in small groups, sheltering under umbrellas and newspapers as best they could. It had been the same at the funeral Mass earlier, and many were already soaked to the bone. They were a hardy breed in these parts though; their stoicism a characteristic acquired early in life. A lifetime spent tending wayward animals and coaxing infertile land saw to that.

By now the vicinity of the grave had become a morass of glue-like soil and it stuck to my shoes in great lumps. There were plenty around with the foresight to wear wellingtons; even Fr Maguire was wearing a pair.

As he finished the prayers mother finally gave way, reaching forward as if to embrace the hole in the ground before collapsing into supporting arms.

'I'd better take her home', said her cousin, several onlookers helping to steer her away for the source of her anguish.

Then I was alone with people filing past me, offering their condolences and shaking my hand. It seemed to go on for a long time. Then Jafe Faulkner was standing before me.

'Saying sorry won't help', he said. 'But I do know how you feel. When my own father died I wanted the earth to swallow me up. So much left unsaid you see…'

I looked at him in surprise. They were the first words we'd exchanged since I was, what?…since I was about twelve. He hadn't changed much that I could see, still as straight as a telegraph pole and as skinny as a whippet. But it was all sinew and muscle; the body of a man who trained and played hard. I was willing to bet that the still ran over the Hill each evening after milking the cows. But then, he probably didn't milk the cows anymore; he had so many other things on his plate now…

'…such a shock to us all. Nobody expected it like that'.

Me least of all. I'd seen him less than a week previously, and, though he's done his usual amount of complaining, he'd shown no outward signs of physical deterioration. Nor had he shown signs subsequently. My mother had woken one morning to find him lying beside her, dead. He had lain down to sleep and not bothered to wake up again.

The day he died had been one long boozing session for me; first celebrating our victory over the company, who had agreed to almost all our demands, and later celebrating Jennifer's birthday at the Cavern. Pissed out of my brain. Jafe was right; so much left unsaid.

I looked at him now, his curly hair glistening in the drizzle. I still didn't like the bastard. Too smooth, too slippery. Well-matched with Bannaher, that was for sure.

'Come over for the send-off', I murmured.

Ritchie had excelled himself, despite the half-finished state of the place. Plates of ham and chicken sandwiches, roast potatoes, mounds of cheese and sliced tomatoes, tiny sausages and bowls of black olives laid out on temporary tables. These were constructed from trestles and sheets of plywood, draped with white sheets. The windows to the extension hadn't yet been fitted, and the openings were shuttered with more sheets of ply. A smell of new wood and creosote hung in the air.

I nursed a large brandy and wondered what the hell I was doing here. I'd been gone, what...six years? It might as well have been sixty so out of place did I feel. Watching people I'd grown up with, gone to school with, others into whose houses I'd wandered as if they had been my own, was like watching strangers. I didn't belong here anymore.

It wasn't a new sensation; I'd felt the same thing once before when I came home on holiday. I had gone to a dance at the Fishermen's Hall in Ross-On - Sea, a venue that I'd always thought of as a palace, only to realise it was nothing more than a glorified shed. I watched from the shadows as a man scattered crystals on the floor - to help the dancers cope with the uneven surface, I guessed. Occasionally, when the hall doubled as a picture hall, the same man had struck terror into us youngsters, curbing our exuberance with whacks on the head from his torch. Now he was just an old man.

Later, as the hall began to fill, I felt like an interloper as I watched an age-old ritual unfold. The men lined up along one wall, the girls along another, the space between a no-man's land where few dared to venture between dances. When the music commenced, it became a buffalo stampede as the men charged across no-man's land to grab the partner they had selected in their minds eye. Sometimes a sharp change of direction was called for to grab a second or third choice.

I hadn't danced all night. I merely stood there and watched, and realised I didn't have the stomach for it anymore. Friends and acquaintances, I watched them waltzing and fox-trotting past me, happy in their world, and I knew I wasn't part of it anymore. Absence hadn't made my heart grow fonder; it had only distanced me from them and their way of life. At that moment I truly understood the expression ' *you can never go back'*, and it almost made me cry

My eyes were drawn to Jafe now, chatting in a quiet corner with one of the wealthier farmers. None of it idle gossip I was willing to wager. Even when he was still a schoolboy, Jafe carried a home-made note-book, meticulously written up in the sloping capitals that were his trademark, indicating where he would be and what he would be doing at any given time during the day.

I saw Ritchie watching him from a distance. A kind of loathing crept across his face, slowly, like a cloud creeping across the sun, darkening it perceptibly. I had never known brothers hate each other so vehemently, and without much care who knew it. Physically, Ritchie was no match for Jafe, but that didn't stop him trying. I remembered the training sessions at the local hurling field, where the practice matches were sometimes wars of attrition, especially on the occasions the brothers were picked on opposing sides. It was just as well they played on the same side in the matches proper, otherwise one of them would never leave the field of play under his own steam. I never knew the reason for their mutual dislike, and I'm not sure Ritchie did either.

'I'm sorry about your father', a voice spoke in my ear. 'I didn't get a chance to say it earlier'.

The speaker was a girl, rather plump in the face, her school-girlish figure suggesting she had not yet shed her puppy fat. She wore her hair in a ponytail, and it was this more than anything that gave her the youthful appearance. On closer inspection I realised she was too old to be a schoolgirl.

'You don't know me, do you?' She spoke again when I failed to answer her. I shook my head.

'Marie Kenny'. She offered her hand, 'Jafe's wife'.

I took her hand.

'You don't say a lot', she continued before I had a chance to reply. 'I was good friends with your brother'.

Jafe's conversation with the big farmer made sense now. Jeremiah Kenny, Geronimo to all who knew him. A nickname that had nothing to do with Indians and everything to do with the blood-curdling cries he made when chasing crows from his cornfields. Marie was his daughter. I remembered her now, not that I ever had much contact with her. She was older than me, Fergus's age in fact, and was already grown-up when I was still at school. She had been away to a boarding convent -without much success I recalled - afterwards spending several years in a sanatorium recovering from an unspecified illness. Subsequently, she remained at home, occasionally frequenting a local dance, but more often than not wandering the fields of her father's not inconsiderable holding.

'My brother?' I couldn't think for a moment. 'Oh yes'.

'We went to school together. I used to watch out for him coming along the Mass path'.

The Mass path. Not much more than a rabbit trail across a couple of fields, but it saved a lot of time compared with going by road. I had used it myself, though in winter it was usually impassable. I often wondered how it had got its name, for it led nowhere near the church.

'I didn't know that', I replied.

'No? Well, you wouldn't remember. We were nearly finished before you began. We're the same age, same birthdays even…I bet you didn't know that?' She smiled when I shook my head. 'You have the same gleam in your eyes. Trouble, I suppose. I remember the time you tried to burn the school down. What made you do it?'

I shrugged.

'Fergus said it was because of the Master'.

'Why would he tell you that?'

'He told me lots of things'.

I looked at her more closely. How friendly had they been?

'The master was a bastard. A sadist too. He beat us up because he enjoyed it. You could see it in his eyes. I spat on his coffin the day he was buried'. I had too. A surreptitious clearing of phlegm from the throat that had landed on the coffin as it was being lowered in to the grave. 'Anyway, it wasn't only me. Fergus and his friends gave him a beating that he never forgot. Jafe too'.

She shook her head. 'Not Jafe. He was too…careful. But I remember it. It was the only thing we talked about for weeks afterwards'.

I remembered it well. Several years after they had finished school, Fergus and a number of others had barricaded him in his classroom during lunch-break, and then kicked the shit out of him. We only found out about it when we filed in for our lessons and found him nursing a bleeding face, with his clothes in tatters. He didn't appear for several days, during which we enjoyed an unexpected break. Not that the beating made much difference; within weeks he was back to his bullying, brutal ways.

He had been particularly vicious towards me during my time at the school, probably because of Fergus, and the memory had lingered with me. I thought I would forget over time, but I hadn't. The humiliation, the sense of hurt, was overpowering at times, and I had often fantasized with Ritchie about how I would get revenge. It was all talk until the night we consumed a flagon of cider between us. We were going to create the biggest blaze Croagh had seen since the time McCarthy's hay-barn had gone up in a ball of flame.

A gallon of paraffin was removed from an outhouse at the Faulkner farm, and as soon as it was dark we staggered in the direction of the school. Ritchie, unfortunately, was in a worse state than me, and fell asleep in a nearby field, leaving me to carry out the deed on my own. That I only managed to set fire to one classroom was due entirely to the effects of the cider; I dropped the container and spilled most of the contents before finally managing sprinkle some. It would have to do I decided, striking a match. Outside again, in the playing fields, I collapsed in a stupor against the perimeter wall, wanting only to sleep. How long I lay there I don't know, but I was roused by shouts coming from the road, and by a crackling noise coming from the school.

I sensed rather than saw Fr Maguire run past me. He came back to stare at me, before running off again. Seeing the blaze had the effect of sobering me up. I realised I was stinking of paraffin. Time to go I knew, and I took off across the fields as fast as my legs would carry me, stopping only to rouse Ritchie.

Fr Maguire came looking for me the next morning. He had the Sergeant with him, and more or less accused me of starting the fire. I brazened it out, saying I was trying to put it out. How come I was smothered in paraffin then? Having got rid of the clothes, I knew he had nothing on me, so I told him he was mistaken. Whether the Sergeant believed it or not, didn't matter; there was nothing he could do without some evidence. I heard no more about it.

''How long have you been married?' I asked Marie.

'Nearly a year''

'He must be a real bundle of fun'.

She laughed, a small tinkling sound. 'I don't kid myself I'm his one great love, if that's what you mean'. She looked over to where he was talking with her father. 'They're probably discussing the price of cattle. I imagine our marriage was arranged like that'. Another tinkle of a laugh. 'I know my father paid him to take me off his hands. Do you think I fetched a good price?'

'You shouldn't put yourself down like that'.

'Why shouldn't I? Anyway, it's true. My brother once said that an old Friesian cow he was sending to the slaughterhouse was more of an asset than me. Speaking as a farmer he was probably right'.

'Speaking as a human being I think it's despicable'.

But then, I wasn't surprised. Land-less farmers' daughters were no good to land-hungry farmers sons. Men had been known to kill for a piece of bog or rock. Land did something to men's minds. Maybe it even affected their sanity. No doubt Marie was right; he had almost certainly received a dowry to take her off her father's hands.

'Fergus always thought a lot of you'. She placed a hand on my arm. 'You're so like him in many ways'.

'How well did you know him?'

'As well as I know my husband'. She looked coolly at me.

I didn't say anything for a moment. Was it possible? She didn't look Fergus's type. But then, who was anybody's type? Was I Tessa's type? I shook my head; there was no clear-cut answer.

Marie mistook my head-shake. 'It's true. It doesn't matter much now I know, but if Fergus was alive today I wouldn't be married to Jafe'.

'Who would you have married...Fergus?'

'The question wouldn't have arisen. I...we were happy the way things were. No one knew about us; it was better that way. It might have been...difficult. He was...'

'From the wrong side of the track?' I finished the sentence when the pause had stretched to several heart-beats.

'I didn't say that'.

'No, you didn't'.

She gave a small shrug. 'People always get the wrong impression, don't they? Fergus and I had something...spiritual. An affinity that went beyond the body. He understood me...my moods...didn't try to change me. And he made me laugh. He was a funny man, your brother, a funny man...' She looked at me with eyes that revealed nothing. 'We talked about going away. Who knows, we might have...'

'Were you happy...was he happy?'

I thought I detected a glimmer of a tear. 'Oh yes, we were very happy'.

'Good. That's some consolation'. I saw Jafe beckoning in our direction. Marie saw him too, and squeezed my arm sympathetically as she took her leave.

'I suppose you knew', I said to Ritchie a few minutes later, as he gave me a refill.

'Knew what?'

'Come on. Don't give me that. You were watching us for the last ten minutes. You fucking knew, didn't you?'

'I knew. But I don't think anyone else did'.

'Not even Jafe?'

'He doesn't notice things like that'.

'Bit futile wasn't it, the two of them? No future in it'.

'Oh, I don't know. It wasn't as if she had anything to bring to the relationship. Land or anything like that. Her father might be a snob, but he's also a realist. When you're desperate, any man is better than no man'. He laughed. 'After all, she married Jafe'.

'I wish I had known him better, but I don't think I knew him at all'.

'Who knows anybody...really? The best we can hope for is to get along with others. As to what makes them tick, well, only they know. Take your father, God rest his soul, how well can you say you knew him?'

I had thought about it. For a long time I had thought about it. In the shithole that was Mousehold, I had lain awake on my bunk many a night trying to understand the enigma that was my father. All those years working at the Mill, cycling there the three miles, come hail, rain or snow. How many million turns of the wheels did that come to? I tried to work it out in my head one night, but had fallen asleep with the question unanswered.

At his retirement party he had been presented with a silver salver and a watch. A picture of himself, being held aloft by a bunch of his work-mates, hung in pride of place in our kitchen.

I shook my head in answer to Ritchie's question. 'He was a stranger to me. And to other people too. When he retired, they gave him an engraved gold watch and a tin tray. And both had his name spelled wrong.

# Chapter seventeen

Bannaher didn't say a word as the project manager gave me the sack. He merely sat there, in his pinstripe suit and his crabby face, a trace of a smile showing as he doodled on the piece of paper that lay on the table in front of him.

Technically, I guess it wasn't the sack. We had all been fired several weeks before, so we could hardly be fired again. But with the strike now settled, the re-employment process had commenced. Selectively, it seemed.

'Barry, isn't it?' The manager looked at his folder again.

'Byrnes. It's Byrnes. As you fucking well know'.

He picked at a pimple on his scabby face. 'Yes, well, looking at your original application, we find a number of inaccuracies on it. It appears that you obtained employment here using false information'. He raised his head and looked at me, a grimace creasing his face, as if he was trying to fart, 'Since then other factors have emerged; imprisonment, deportation, need I go on...?'

'You need', I replied, looking at Bannaher.

He shook his head. 'This company has a reputation to protect. We simply cannot afford to employ... people like you'.

*People like me?* Now where had I heard that phrase before? I lost my rag.

'It's him, isn't it? He turned you against me. That bastard. Just like he's trod on the backs of good men in Kilburn, he's trying to do the same here...' I was halfway across the table, halfway to getting my hands round Bannaher's throat and squeezing till his eyes popped out, when hands grabbed me and bundled me out of the office. Somebody cuffed me on the head, and when the ringing in my ears had stopped I was sitting on the kerb some fifty yards from the office.

Tom Whyte was looking anxiously at me.

'You look like you could do with a brandy', he said. 'Come on'.

'Here's to people like me', I said as the Hennessy hit bedrock.

'Like us. I got the push too'.

'*There's no job here for people like you*, that's what the scabby bastard said to me. What am I, a leper or something?'

'It's not the only job in the world'.

I laughed. 'A few months ago I couldn't have given a shit. Christ, I haven't done more than a couple of months work in the last five years. But I really thought this time I was leaving the bad old days behind. I was getting into it, you know? Really getting into it. And now this...'

'The bums rush? The soldier's farewell? Me, I never expect too much - and I am seldom disappointed. It's only a fucking job, and a crappy one at that'.

'You don't seem too upset'.

'Oh, I am. But not at the company. After all, they're the enemy. The visible one, anyway. I only got what I expected. The union, now, they're a different kettle of fish-heads. For them to agree to a deal which gave them their rises in return for selective re-employment was... well, we were fucking sold out'.

'You think they knew who was for the chop?'

''Course they fucking knew. That's how things are done. The company was giving something, they wanted something in return. That old quid pro pro. Getting rid of so-called troublemakers is also sending a signal to the rest - toe the line or else!' He paused. 'Though I can't figure out how you fit in there. Maybe they found out you were one of those that tipped the van into the canal'.

I shook my head. 'That wasn't it. I saw an old friend in there'. I expounded a little on my acquaintance with Bannaher. 'He marked their card, so as to speak. Though I don't know what he was doing there'

'Wonder no more. He's the new owner'.

-

When Jennifer turned up I wasn't quite legless, but I was getting there.

'What will you do?' she asked.

'Get out of this one-horse town'. I stifled a burp and laughed instead. 'There's a new Marshal in town that don't like me'. I sniggered. 'Marshal Bannaher'.

Whyte, who had lain slumped in his seat for the last half-hour, stood up suddenly.

'Bang, bang', he shouted, arm extended, index finger pointing. 'Bannaher will pick you off, one by one. The only good worker is a frightened one'.

'Hey Sitting Bull, why don't you put a sock in it? If it hadn't been for you we wouldn't have lost our jobs in the first place'.

I looked to see where the voice came from. It was Martin, one of the trenchers, who a few weeks ago, had been to the forefront on the picket line.

'Judas sold out for twenty pieces of silver, you did it for a lot less...'

'You watch your mouth...'

'If you had any decency, you'd have told them where to stick their jobs. One out all out, one for all... isn't that the way it's supposed to be...?'

Whyte held up his hand. 'Fair's fair, Terry. Martin has a point, let him have his say'.

Martin stood up. 'You can keep your fancy talk, Whyte. We know all about your carry-on in London. Many a good man lost his job because of you. Well, it's not going to happen here. You lot are nothing but communists and anarchists'. Emboldened by the hum of approval, he raised his voice. 'Taking the bread out of the mouths of children, that's what you're doing'.

There was silence for a moment. When Whyte replied there was a sarcastic edge to the words. 'And how many children have you got?'

'None'.

'None'. He nodded his head as he spoke. 'But you own fifty acres of land. Or is it sixty? You send milk to the creamery, you sow grain crops, you buy and sell animals at the mart. You are what is euphemistically called a small farmer. You survived on the land before this job came along, you'll survive after it's gone. Your wife is a nurse, your father a tillage contractor'. He paused and looked around him. 'There are many, many unemployed men around this town who haven't got fifty fucking acres to fall back on when times get tough. So tell me again who is taking the bread out of the mouths of children'.

After that things went rapidly downhill. Martin, raging that he had been made to look a fool, clambered over a table to get to Whyte, but slipped and crashed into another one, sending pints and shorts skittering in all directions. Soon there were arguments raging in every corner of the bar, and Jango was rushing about picking up stools and trying to placate everyone. Whyte grinned at me as he slipped out the fire door.

'Come on', Jennifer dragged me the same way.

Later, stretched out on her settee with coffee and cigarettes, I watched as she banged away on her typewriter.

'What's the story?' I asked.

'Man bites dog then bites himself'. She laughed at her little joke. 'I thought a few paragraphs about the bad feeling that exists between the two groups - those re-employed and those not - might interest our readers'.

'They are your readers'. I paused. 'You can't write about that'.

'Why not? It's still a free country'.

'I didn't mean it that way. I...look, there's only two...Whyte and me. The rest were all taken back'.

'I know that'.

'We'll be branded as troublemakers'.

'Are you telling me you care? The guy who lists prison and deportation amongst his pastimes?'

'Who told you that stuff?'

'You're not denying it then?'

I shrugged. 'Not much point is there? You're the newshound. You could easily verify it'.

She pushed her chair back from the desk and held out her hand. I passed the cigarette to her.

'A dark horse is how my mother would describe you. Whenever something secret was discovered about someone in our neighbourhood, that's what she said. '*He's a dark horse, that fella*'.

'So how did you find out?'

She passed the cigarette back, blowing a thin stream of smoke between her pursed lips, then reached over and passed me a thin file.

'It was pushed under my door earlier today'.

I read it in silence; a neatly-typed dossier of most of my activities in London, and all of it accurate too. Park Royal and the walkie-talkies, the thefts from the jewelers, robbing the pubs, jail and deportation - it was all there.

I handed it back. 'Impressive'.

'And true?' Her face was impassive; nothing in there to indicate she cared one way or the other.

I shrugged again. 'More or less'.

'Why would somebody send it to me?'

'You're a reporter'. I laughed. 'And you must admit it makes better reading than the prices heifers fetched at the fair in Kilmallock yesterday'.

'Have you any idea who's behind it?'

'Not just an idea. He may not actually have typed it himself, but then you don't pull the cart when you've got an ass to do it'.

'Your friend Bannaher I take it'.

'Who else? He's the only one who knows all that stuff. Well no, that's not strictly true. There's a few more, but he's the only one who would be bothered to use it in this way'.

'What's behind it Terry? What's he got against you?'

I shook my head. 'I wish I knew. I honest-to-God-don't-know. Maybe it's my boyish good looks - he's a crabby ould fucker himself'. I took a sip from the coffee and made a face. 'Have you anything stronger than this? Something to deaden the pain?'

She stood up and rummaged for a few minutes, returning with a bottle of Cherry Brandy.

'Here we are, the last of my Christmas leftovers'.

I tried some and made a face. 'Christ, your Christmas party must have been a howl'.

She laughed. 'It was for the gate-crashers. They didn't stay long'. We made ourselves comfortable on the floor, sitting back-to-back on the carpet. I could feel her bra-stays digging into my back.

'I really know nothing about you', she said after a silence had grown.

I didn't reply. Tessa would have supplied all the information, what he didn't know himself that is. She might even have typed the fucking thing for him. Why would he go to all that trouble? Christ, I hadn't set eyes on the bastard for all of two years. And then only briefly in that hotel in Manchester. We'd argued and I had left, but it couldn't have been because of that. We hardly knew each other anyway. Sure, our paths had crossed over the years, but only briefly. I doubted if I was important enough to warrant such close attention. A welder on a poxy construction site...what kind of threat did that pose? Yet he clearly didn't want me around...

'Are you listening?' Jennifer nudged me in the ribs.

'Sorry, did I miss something?'

'I said...I know nothing about you'.

'Nor I you. Who knows anything about anybody?'

She swung around quickly, so quickly that I almost fell over. My drink didn't fare so well, half of it splashing on the carpet.

'Leave it!', she said angrily as I began to rise. 'This is me, Terry...what you see. No hidden extras. Twenty three years of age, left school at eighteen, started on the paper at nineteen. No weddings, no divorces, no criminal record, and my teeth are all my own. Now you know all about me'.

'You forgot about the singing'.

'Okay...' she shouted...'so I forgot the singing. Betty and the Bees. Five years on the local scene and starting to make a name for ourselves. That's it. That's absolutely it.' She fluttered a hand in agitation. 'But you...your CV reads like something out of...out of Crime Monthly'.

'It does, doesn't it?'

She elbowed me again. 'Are you going to tell me?'

I held up my hands. 'Alright. What do you want to know?'

'Everything'.

'This might take some time'. I settled myself more comfortably, this time with my back against the settee. 'Let's see...I left school when I was fourteen - no, thirteen - I began working when I was fourteen. Nothing special, assisting a van-man on his rounds. Still, it was better than working for some fucking farmer…'

'Hold it! What have you got against farmers? For all you know I might be a farmer's daughter'.

'Are you?'

'No'.

'Then take my word for it. Being a farm worker isn't much better than being a slave. We can spend all night talking about farmers if you like'.

She shook her head. 'Carry on'.

'I lasted a long time with the van-man considering - almost six months. He couldn't keep his hands to himself; every time he got a chance he was trying to get my trousers down. Then laughing it off as a joke when I got mad. I might have been green, but I wasn't that green'.

'That's awful. Didn't you tell anyone?'

I shook my head. Who could I tell? The Sergeant? He'd laugh me out of the barracks and say that whatever I got I deserved. Fr Maguire? That his own sacristan was prone to pulling his wire out and sticking it under my nose whenever the fancy took him? I didn't think so. When I couldn't take it any longer I grabbed at his big dangling pair of balls one morning and squeezed so hard he passed out. He was off work for a week and I was looking for another job.

'I sorted it out myself. After that I did whatever work came along. A spell in the woods felling timber. Harvesting. I even helped out on a fishing boat for a while. Then when I was sixteen I got a job in the mill with father. My name was down for a long time, and I knew that as soon as I was old enough, and a job was going, I would be called'. I laughed. 'Fatherly influence'.

'Fergus never worked in the mill?'

'No. I think the place was in the doldrums for a long time. And when jobs finally came along he had a job that he liked. And was good at. Besides, he was the outdoor type - he wouldn't have been suited to the mill at all'. I laughed. 'Not that I was either'.

'You miss him, don't you?'

Jesus, did I miss him. 'I could look up to him, see? When I was growing up. There was no one else I could do that to. He was so…steadfast, you know. And yet there was…something…I don't know. He could be…that's it, unpredictable'. I paused, remembering. 'He used to play the trumpet at one time'.

'He was a musician?'

'He would have liked to have been, I think. I remember him and a few friends practising in our shed. They were very good I think. They may even have played one or two gigs. Then they broke up; one or two emigrated - although Fergus continued to play the trumpet though for a while after'. I could almost see him now, sitting halfway up our hill, under the setting sun, playing The Legions Last Patrol. The crisp, clear notes hung in the air for an age before fading away, a sound so lonesome it almost made you cry. Then without warning he packed it all up, sold the trumpet, never played a note again. I never found out why.

Jennifer got out her cigarettes and we lit up, smoking companionably for a few moments.

'Life at the Mill was a bastard', I continued. 'After the novelty wore off. Clocking on, clocking off, and in between times standing beside a clacking machine all day, packing bags of flour, the noise from the big crushers on the floor above grinding away in your head, slowly driving you mad'.

'That was what I was expected to do for the next forty years. My life... not only do it, but actually appreciate it. It was good enough for the likes of my father, why shouldn't it be good enough for me? And, as I was constantly reminded, it was a steady job. Oh yes, it was all mapped out for me; the job, a house, a wife, mini-versions of me...the whole shebang'. I laughed. 'Only, I wasn't very good at map-reading'.

'About this time, I began to acquire a bit of a reputation. Anything that happened, I was usually connected with it. A few of us, you know?...just pranks at first, but it got us noticed. Father said I was mixing with the wrong crowd, that they were having a bad influence on me. But I was the bad influence. I was the instigator'. I laughed. 'That was the name my friends stuck on me - The Instigator. It came about after we smoked a couple of old bachelors out of their home by blocking the chimney with sacks. Fr Maguire said at Mass the following Sunday that the instigator should be horse-whipped, and the name stuck. Then I tried to burn the school down of course, and Fr Maguire knew it. Even he referred to me as the instigator after that'.

'The job at the mill was supposed to quieten me down, make a man of me, but it did neither. I bought myself a motorbike, a little Honda machine, and tried hill-climbing with it...' I looked at Jennifer...'you've seen some of our hills. Anyway, we started using them as scrambling tracks. Which didn't go down very well with the sheep - or the farmers who owned them. The Sergeant was called in, and gave to chasing us. He never got within an asses roar of me, until one day I misjudged things and ended up in a ravine. It was the end of the bike...and very nearly the end of me. It took me six months to recover, and by then I had no job to return to'.

'I wasn't worried, but father was, so to keep the peace I went to the mill manager and begged for my job back. It was no use, he wasn't about to give me a second chance. I saw red - I had been forced to beg for a job I didn't want - so a few nights later I sabotaged a lot of the machinery. It was easy. It was the middle of the night, and there was no one about. It was smack in the middle of the harvest season, and it took the mill nearly two weeks to get back in business. They lost a lot of custom that year'.

Jennifer's mouth was open. 'You're making it up!'

I laughed. 'You wanted the full story and this is it. The gospel according to St Terry. You see why I had to get away? There was no place for me in Croagh anymore. Besides, I couldn't stand the sight of the place any longer. Every time I passed the barracks, Sergeant Cronin was there, watching and waiting. Waiting for me to slip up. There was only one place to go'.

'How many Irish have said that over the years!'

'Plenty. You've no idea how different London is. You can be whoever you like, live the way you want, and nobody cares a damn. You don't have to get up in the morning if you don't want to, don't have to go to Mass on Sunday...'

'I like going to Mass on Sunday'.

'It's a free country is all I'm saying. You don't have to be hypocritical about it. Here, if you don't go, you can be sure someone will remark on it. Over there, nobody gives a damn'.

'Sign's on it's such a pagan place'.

'You sound like my mother'. Then I saw she was laughing at me. 'Anyway, I wound up in that pagan place. And went from bad to worse'. I picked up the dossier then dropped it again. 'The rest you know'.

She stood up and pressed the wrinkles from her skirt. 'What now?'

I shrugged. 'Who knows? I'll probably go back'.

'But you've been deported...'

'So?' I stood up myself. I had a feeling I wasn't going to get much more here tonight. Besides, the effects from my earlier drinking session had just about knackered me. 'Anyway, there's not much to keep me here now'.

She didn't speak for a moment. 'Isn't there? Only you can answer that'.

When I didn't reply she reached down and retrieved the dossier. 'I won't use any of this. It's nobody's business but yours'. She held it out to me. 'Take it'.

When I didn't, she threw it on the settee. I could see the exasperation on her face. 'Look, I know it's none of my business, but when are you going to stop running away?'

I snorted. ' Me running away! From what?'

'I don't know. Yourself…responsibility…life. I could name a dozen reasons and all of them could be right'.

'Or none of them'.

'Is that what you really think?'

'Maybe I'm just unlucky'.

'See what I mean? Everything's just a laugh, isn't it?'

Maybe she was right. But I just couldn't take another bout of psychoanalysis. I'd had all the Freudian mumbo-jumbo I could stomach. I didn't care anymore what the reasons were. Things just happened it seemed. And there wasn't a lot you could do about most of them.

I wasn't laughing as I let myself out. The rain was slanting down, beating a tattoo on the slate roofs and the cobbled walkways, the streetlights opaque in the background. Limerick rain was always wet rain. I pulled my collar up and started to run. As I lengthened my stride I could hear the shouts behind me; 'Terry, come back, you'll catch your death'.

# Chapter eighteen

Oh Christ. My life is one big fuck-up. *Most people's lives are shit,* wasn't that what Tessa said to me. Not hers though. No not Tessa's. She took a pull on that old fruit machine of life and came away with the jackpot. What had she been like on the game, I wondered? Did she wank guys off, suck their cocks, take it up the back? I guess she did. It was all part of the trade. The oldest trade in the world.

Tessa and her pimp. Fucking pimp Chris. Good old Chris, procuring for his own sister. How much of a cut did you take Chris? Maybe you did it for brotherly love. That hundred pounds she'd wangled off me in Brighton had been one of your brainwaves no doubt. You cunt.

She saw me coming a mile off. No, ten miles. And yet there had been a time when she felt something for me. I couldn't have been that wrong. She couldn't have been that good an actress.

The trouble with women like Tessa is that they are always available to the highest bidder. They may not always prostitute themselves in the conventional manner, but the for-sale sign is pretty obvious nevertheless. Love doesn't come into it. Or if it does it's of a narcissistic nature. They only person those bitches love is themselves. They love their flat bellies, their perfect breasts, their even tans, the aren't-I-gorgeous aura they surround themselves with. How else could they justify the bizarre and grotesque couplings they engage in? Bannaher was no oil painting, but even he was an Adonis compared to some of the hound-dogs I had seen limping into the sunset with their own Barbie Doll in tow.

All women were whores. It was their nature. My own mother included. She was selling the house. Our home. My home. No, it wasn't my home. It had never really been that for a long time. Not for as long as I cared to remember. I had never been much more than a lodger at that address. And yet it bothered me.

I suppose it's hard to deny your roots and - despite everything - I had grown up there. And bits of me stayed there. In the hedgerows, in the pine groves, in the Mass-path, and in that bloody hill. It had possessed my young soul and my growing body - and now it was being sold.

I felt like a man without a country. Here I was, turfed out of the flat in Limerick because I no longer had a job with the company, and now I was being told there was no room for me at home either. No room at the inn as it were.

The house had been locked and I had found mother at her cousin's place, an old thatched cottage on the cliffs, overlooking Ross-On-Sea. Widowed herself, she eked out a living selling dilisk, and letting the solitary caravan adjacent to the cottage. Sometimes campers pitched their tents on her half-acre, bringing in a few extra pounds. Across the bay Bannaher's holiday complex was rising inexorably along the shoreline.

'I suppose you'll be heading back to London so', mother said, after telling me the good news. 'There's nothing to keep you around here now, is there?'

When I got over the shock I told her she couldn't sell it. 'But it's your home. Our home. Father wouldn't want you to sell it'.

'Your father no longer cares, God rest his soul. It's because of it he is where he is. I couldn't live there now, with all that I cherish gone'.

It was my first clear indication that she had no great regard for me. Mother-love had never been one of her more notable qualities, but I had put it down to her rather dour nature. Not once did I remember her putting her arms around me and giving me the kind of hugs mothers are supposed to. Oh, she wiped my nose and combed my hair and fixed the grazes on my knees, but I never remembered her kissing anything better. Even when I saw other mothers fussing and clucking over their children, it never registered. She was my mother, and mothers were notoriously odd creatures. Now there it was, staring me plain in the face; she didn't like me; she never had.

'You still have me'.

'Have I?' She looked at me with eyes brimming with sadness and bewilderment. 'You went from me a long time ago, boy'.

'Where will you live?' I asked, more to cover my own sadness than anything else, although I was pretty sure I knew the answer.

'Where do you think but here? If you can't turn to your own flesh and blood in times of need who can you turn to?'

It didn't occur to her that I was her own flesh and blood.

'And the extra money means that we can both enjoy a little comfort at long last'.

'Indeed we will'. Her cousin, who was the elder by several years, and who had been on her own for the last ten of them, would probably be glad of the company. Any company, even that of a cousin you didn't always see eye to eye with, was better than none when you had been alone for so long. 'Sure, thirty thousand can buy you a lot of comfort'.

'Thirty thousand!', I managed when I had recovered. 'Who in his right mind would pay that kind of money?'

'That's what the fella offered me. The solicitor advised me to take it. He said I wouldn't get an offer like it again'.

'Take it you fool, take it!, I says to her. And throw me in as well', her cousin cackled. 'For that amount of money I'd a bitten his hand off'.

'Hold on, what fella? Tell me his name and I'll find out what asylum he escaped from'.

'He's no lunatic. They say he has tubs of money'. Mother waved her hand in the general direction of the bay. 'Him. That fella building the big hotel over there'.

-

'So there you have it', I said. 'That bastard now owns the bloody bed I used to sleep in '.

Whyte took a long pull at his Guinness, wiping the sliver of moustache on the back of his hand afterwards.

'I'd say now...' he paused to take a drag on his fag...' that in this instance you're right. He wanted you out of the way - or so pre-occupied - that you wouldn't stop to think what was going on. He was probably hoping you'd piss off back to the Smoke and not find out about the sale until it was too late'.

'It's too late now. And what do you mean by 'in this instance'?'

'Aw come on, Terry. You have a persecution complex as far as that fucker is concerned.'.

'Complex me arse. Everywhere I turn, he's there. That can't be co-incidence'.

'And why not? You and I both know the construction industry isn't that big. The same faces keep turning up on job after job. We're all fishes in the same pool. He's just a bigger fish than most'.

'He's a fucking shark. Or a piranha'.

Finding Whyte hadn't been difficult. Having established from Jango that he was still around town, I merely sat in the bar till he put in an appearance. The news was bad; he was blacklisted on every building site in the city. If he wanted a job he'd have to change his name, maybe even his colour.

'They can't operate a blacklist', I protested. 'It must be against some law'.

'They can do what they like. It's not written in tablets of stone...oh no, that would be discrimination...but when it's written in the hearts and the minds, well, it might just as well be'. He grinned. 'Let's face it, you and I are bad news in this town, boy'.

'In more ways than one. Jennifer's given me the elbow'.

'I thought you were well in there'.

'So did I'.

'So what did you do to blot the old copybook?'

'Not too sure. I may have hinted I was considering going back to London...'

'There you go then'.

'It wasn't serious or anything. Neither of us had made any commitments or promises'.

He wagged a finger. 'That's the trouble you see. She may have read more into it than you think. White dresses, pink carnations, wedding bells, that sort of thing'. He grinned. 'That's the crux of it. I'd say'.

'We never spoke of anything like that'.

'That wouldn't stop her thinking about it. You know the way women's minds work. Then you go and mention you might be leaving...'

'She knows too much about me. Knows what I'm like only too well...hell, you know most of it too. Why would she want to take on that burden?'

'There isn't a woman born who doesn't believe she can change a man...make him mend his ways'.

'But it was all good fun. We had a laugh, a drink, and...you know'.

'Sounds to me like she was measuring you for the suit. Then the ring appears and - snap, the manacles are on. Had she brought you home to see mammy and daddy by any chance?'

'No'

'You got out just in time. If you're not the marrying kind, I mean'. When I didn't reply he clapped me on the shoulder. 'Come back for a bite to eat. There's something I want to show you'.

His place was a rundown cottage, just off the Ennis road, about four miles from the city. It was a combination of garish colours, the most prominent of which was a disgusting-looking sort of lilac.

'A job lot?' I enquired as we drove past a pair of purple piers with gold balls on top. 'Or was the painter just colour-blind?'

'Neither. My wife. You'll like her'.

Hens and ducks scattered as we stuttered to a halt. In the background I could see a tethered goat grazing, and by the rear fence a similarly tied donkey.

'Welcome to my smallholding'. He pulled a lever and the bonnet of the pick-up shot up, leaving a plume of steam in its wake. 'Or should I say my wife's'. A tall, blonde woman had appeared in the doorway, a paint-daubed smock her most noticeable garment. 'It's Toni's money - and talent - that keeps the wolf from the door'.

'Hi', we shook hands, hers slightly sweaty. 'It's Antonia actually. He calls me Toni'. She laughed. 'It could be worse, it could be Tone'.

'Which do you prefer?'

She shrugged. 'Most of his friends call me Toni...now'. She looked about thirty five, fresh-faced and was - to my surprise - English. Her accent was decidedly twangy though, not London I thought. Definitely not East End.

'I'll call you that then'.

'Fine'. She waved a hand vaguely. 'You'll have to forgive the mess. We haven't been here that long'.

'Long enough'. Whyte raised his head from beneath the bonnet. 'This bloody water pump's had it. She's a painter, and you know how untidy they are'.

'House painter?'

She laughed at my suggestion. 'You've noticed the colour scheme then? It was an experiment that went...slightly wrong'.

'So was Frankenstein's monster'. This was Whyte.

'I paint sports cars. Mazzerati's, Aston Martins, MG'S, you name in'.

'In there?' Indicated the house. 'Bit cramped isn't it?'

'No you fool, on canvas'.

Whyte slammed the bonnet down. 'Take no notice of him. He's only taking the Michael'.

'Not much of a market around here for that sort of thing, is there?' Jango's doggy sculptures came to mind as I spoke. I couldn't see canvas cars sitting easily in the average Limerick sitting room either.

She shook her head. 'I have a friend who has a gallery in Brighton. He sells what he can'.

Brighton. Now that was more like it. Was she a Brighton belle?

'Nice town. Are you a native?'

'I went to University there. An arts degree'.

'Not teaching then?'

'I was. I mean, I used to'. Her hand encompassed the house and the several acres that comprised the smallholding. 'This is my revenge on it all. I've had my fill of pimply students and warty old heads'.

'We're drop-outs', Whyte explained when we had adjourned to the kitchen, 'from the whole fucking mess'. He indicated the array of food on the table;

bread, eggs, bowls of vegetables and salad. 'All our own produce. We're self-sufficient here - or as much as we can be'. He helped himself to some food, indicating I should do the same. 'We've been here nearly six months now, gradually licking the place into shape. It's hard work though...and it takes money'.

I was beginning to see. 'Which is why...'

'Which is why I was working on that fucking pipeline. A few more months and we were home free'.

'Why rock the boat then?'

'I didn't. Not in the beginning. Then that Moynihan turned up and twigged who I was. I knew it was all up then. When Jimmy broke his leg I had to create a diversion. It was what Moynihan would have expected from me. He knew me from London, knew what I was like'.

Toni poured some tea. 'Had been, dear. That was ages ago'.

I laughed. 'He did mention something about anarchists and the like'.

'All history now. I'm a reformed character these days'. He took Toni's hand. 'Two years, isn't it Toni? We're kindred spirits. Toni also had grief where she worked. Willesden High - a big school run by little minds. Trying to organise the labour there, working to improve teachers conditions, was a nightmare. In the end she was hounded out. We decided that a new start, a new approach to life, was the only way'.

'Pity you broke that driver's jaw then'.

'Some things you can't change. Besides, he had it coming. For all the reasons I mentioned before. But there was another reason; I knew him from London too. And a more racist, anti-Irish, anti-anyone-not-English bastard you never saw. National Front merchant. If he and his kind had their way we'd all be building our own gas-chambers. All I can say is that he's lucky he got out of town in one piece'.

'Tom's not half as bad as he's been painted'. Toni refilled our mugs.

'What else did Moynihan say about me?'

'Oh...enough'.

'Believe nothing you hear - and only half what you see, that's my philosophy'.

'Where do you go from here?'

He shrugged. 'Something will turn up. It always has. I never starved a winter yet. There's plenty out there that know me. Someone might need a barn rebuilding, or a tree knocking down'.

'For a guy who hasn't been here that long, you know a lot of people'. I knew that he was from Galway, and had been surprised when, on the way out from Limerick, he had kept up a running conversation; *'see that farm there? I piked hay there...lovely girl the daughter. That house on the hill...old Dinny Reilly had that...left it to a nephew, along with twenty acres of furze bushes. That galvanised shed in that field there...the locals built that for the Bishop...he cremated himself one night, along with a packet of Woodbines...used to sleep in a tar-barrel before that'...'*

He laughed now and slapped his thigh. 'I mightn't have went to school, but I met the scholars, that's what my old man used to say. The egg man they called him. Well why wouldn't they? He bought eggs from half the country. When I wasn't at school, which was fairly often, I travelled round with him. I know more people than ten parish priests put together'. He paused and was silent for a moment. 'Twenty years of buying and selling eggs gave him enough to buy a grocery shop cum pub in the village. I think that what drove him on was the thought of them all laughing at him; *'Where's the money in eggs?'* they'd laugh. *'Six children to feed and not two pennies to rub together...you'd be better off on the dole'.* Well, he proved them wrong and it killed him. Five years in the pub and he drank himself to death'.

After the meal the three of us wandered round the smallholding. One plot was devoted to vegetables; lettuce, carrots, spring onions, cabbages and several greens that I couldn't put a name to.

'My contribution to the enterprise', he informed me. 'Organically grown. We flog what we don't need'.

Toni's studio was a lean-to tacked onto the gable end of the house. Most of the pictures in view were landscapes; delicate water-colours of farmers and fishermen working at their crafts, ones attention cleverly drawn to a point where the colours suddenly exploded like a firework on Guy Fawlkes night.

'These are good, but I thought you painted cars', I said.

'For profit. These are for pleasure'. In one corner was a stack of canvasses covered with a paint-spattered sheet. She removed the sheet. 'These are what I prostitute my talent on'.

I could see where the house colours came from. Lurid, mechanised monsters seemed about to leap through the canvas at me. The menace, the feeling of controlled power, the suggestion of awesome power were captured to perfection in every brush stroke. She was good.

'Impressive. Do you sell many?'

'On a good month, one'.

'And a bad month?'

'Don't depress me'.

Whyte had been pulling at a block in the end wall. It came away to reveal a cavity.

'I suppose you're wondering why I brought you out here?' His hand reached in and came out with a greaseproof package. He placed the package on the table and unwrapped it. 'What do you think of these beauties?'

My first reaction was to step back. 'Gelignite?'

'Dynamite. Relax, it's as safe as houses. You could throw this stuff on a fire and all it would do is burn'. He smiled. 'With the detonators of course it's a different matter. And those...' he smiled again...' are in another safe place'.

'The rumour was true after all, then'.

'What rumour is that? There've been so many'.

'That you had got hold of some explosives on a demolition site...' I looked at him aghast....'My god, you brought them all the way back here!'

He shook his head again and smiled at me. 'Not me'.

Toni was smiling now. 'They would never think a woman would be that crazy'.

'But why? Why risk it? You could have got ten years'.

'More. But there really wasn't much risk. More chance of getting run over crossing the road'.

I shook my head. I had done many wild things myself, but transporting dynamite hundreds of miles would never be one of them. Not in a million years.

'Why tell me? I mean it's dangerous...the more people that know...'

She laughed. 'You won't tell. And we thought...well, it might interest you. Go on Tom, you tell him...'

Whyte looked at me. 'You know this trouble with Bannaher...how much would you say he owed you?'

'A lot'.

'Ten thousand? Fifteen? Five grand each. We could do with the money, and I'm sure you could too'. He picked up one of the sticks and held it aloft. 'We've got the power...how about it?'

'Extortion? We're talking extortion?'

'Let's call it friendly persuasion'.

'You know what I think? You're fucking mad the pair of you'.

# Chapter nineteen

We watched from a pine grove a hundred yards away as the Mercedes pulled up by Crowley's field. Bannaher looked around for a moment, then opened the gate and stepped inside. We knew what he would find; an exposed section of pipe, covered temporarily with a piece of plywood. Taped to the pipe was a candle and a scrawled message; 'see how easy it is'.

'Who's that with him?' Whyte handed me the glasses.

I searched for a glimpse of his companion's face. *Turn round you bastard. That's better you whore's melt.* 'It's the site manager'.

His relief was audible. 'No police then'.

'Didn't I tell you that? Not his style. He likes to see to things himself''. As I knew to my cost in that shithole he called a club.

'That's what I like about you, Terry...you don't believe in fuck-all anymore'. He laughed. 'Maybe you never did? Me, I was a true believer...once. Oh yes. I embraced more 'isms' than Valentino did women. And all I ever got was heartache. There's always plenty willing to load the bullets for you, but when it comes to firing the gun, guess who gets lumbered every time? Now I'm embracing a new 'ism'...every-man-for-himself-ism'.

'Good. Now get off your soapbox and let's go. They're leaving'.

Despite my better judgment - or maybe because I never had any - I had decided to go along with my new-found dynamite-toting friends. The scheme, if unsuccessful, could get us all a ten stretch, so I wasn't about to go hare-brained about it. I didn't know about Mountjoy, but if it was half as bad as Wandsworth then I wasn't about to apply for lodgings there. Not if I could help it.

Our first conference had centred round the aims of the group - and the best way of achieving them. 'It has to be run like a military operation', Toni said, 'and worked out to the very last degree. We can't afford any slip-ups'. She slipped into the role of organiser so easily that I could see she must have been a demon at Willesden High.

We thought about how best to pressurise Bannaher so that he had no choice but to pay. The holiday complex was well above ground by now, but the holiday season was in full swing and it would be difficult to get into the site without being noticed. Besides, if the worst came to the worst, we didn't want any innocent bystanders involved. There was the batching plant behind our hill - no, his hill now - now in full swing, but, again, very difficult to gain access to. By far the best option was the pipeline; miles and miles of open countryside and hardly a human in sight.

Our first communication with Bannaher was at the hotel he was staying at in Limerick. For some reason he was not yet living at Ross House, although with Tessa in residence Fr Maguire would probably take a dim view. *'Better wait till after the wedding, Pat, you know how people talk.'*

The brown envelope had contained a stick of dynamite, various photos of the pipeline (Toni's handiwork with her Polaroid), and a letter which read; *'There's more of this stuff waiting to blow lots of holes in your pipeline. If you doubt it, go and inspect the section at Crowley's field. (look it up on your drawings) Oh, and get £15,000 ready, then wait for further instructions. No cops or all bets are off'.*

The letter had been compiled using the text from several newspapers, cut out and laboriously pasted by Toni. All of which prompted Whyte to suggest that she had been watching too many films. Personally I thought she had been reading too many Micky Spillane books.

'He's bitten', I said to her after we returned from Crowley's field. 'Now for phase two'.

'First we let him sweat a little. We may as well get our money's worth out of the bastard'.

I had been amazed at the speed that Toni decided to dislike him. She didn't know him, had never set eyes on him, had only my account of my run-ins with him on which to make a judgement. And I could have been lying my head off. It was as if she had been looking for an enemy; someone to lock horns with. There were people like that; she struck me as the type who would always need a cause to fight for. Stagnating in the wilds of Limerick didn't seem her, somehow. Then, it wasn't me either. But we didn't always have a choice in these matters.

Maybe I should just have walked away from all this madness in the first place. And it was madness. I knew that, despite my going along with it. I mean…explosives and extortion! It wasn't me at all. It was more the action of terrorists than villains. Did that make me a terrorist?

I laughed at my misgivings. There were a lot of barriers I was prepared to leap to get my revenge on Bannaher. Since my mother revealed his purchase of the house I had been back several times; mainly to visit the cemetery. Trying to talk to father in death wasn't any easier than it had been in life. He was still reproaching me I felt, still telling me I would come to a sticky end. Still disappointed in me.

154

Later, in the pub, Ritchie seemed surprised that I hadn't held out for more for the house.

'Jafe has been crowing about what a bargain they got. Your half of the hill, I mean'.

'It wasn't my half, it was mother's. I knew nothing about the deal'.

When I outlined the circumstances he sounded incredulous. 'You got nothing!'

'Not a sausage. Mother hasn't offered anything, and I haven't asked'.

'No wonder they're crowing. The irony is they got it for a song when you think about it. They'll probably make thirty million on the deal'.

'Come again?'

'I said, thirty million. I've done a quick calculation based on a similar operation the other side of the county. It's probably got a thirty-year life-span, your hill. When they get properly set up, and the wagons start rolling in earnest, they should gross a million a year. One thousand pounds per annum, that's all it will have cost them'.

Trust Ritchie to have it all worked out. Maths had always been his strong point. Not that it was much consolation to me that I had just seen my retirement money go up in smoke. Thirty million...how could it be? I didn't doubt Ritchie's sums; I just couldn't figure out how it could come to so much. But then, thirty million was just a number - it didn't mean anything to me - and thirty years was a long way down the road. Still, it meant Bannaher shouldn't have any problems raising the money.

We had already selected where the drop would be made. In the foothills behind the village of Murroe. At the top of a long, straight climb that afforded a panoramic view of the countryside spread out below. And with a clear sight of anyone following along behind.

Bannaher didn't know the exact location; all he had been furnished with was a map of the area, and instructions to carry on driving until he came to a blue light in the middle of the road. ('a bit melodramatic', I'd said to Whyte. 'It'll have to do', he'd replied, showing me the old ambulance siren he had been working on. ''It's all we have'.) He was to leave the money by the light, in a hold-all, then head back the way he had come.

It was all forestry land up here. Most of it had been planted with trees, great tracts of pine and spruce blanketing the hillsides. Whyte had remembered it from years ago, when he had worked there for a summer, cutting down trees for the chipboard factory in Scarrif. It had been back-breaking work because most of the wood had blown down in earlier storms, which had left large areas of forest one, tangled mass. They had to cut it into manageable lengths then haul it down the hillside to the roadside, where it was loaded onto lorries and transported to the factory.

'It's the ideal spot, believe me. Only one way in by car...and you can see for miles. But there's dozens of trails...' he waved at the hills behind him... 'that will take a motorbike. We'll be indoors before they realise we've picked up the money'.

It was almost dusk as we watched the car make its way slowly up the incline.

I looked at my watch. 'On time anyhow'.

Whyte set the blue light in the middle of the road and switched it on. An eerie glow lit up the half-light.

'It'll be seen for miles around', I said.

'Maybe they'll think it's a knocking shop. One of those mobile ones'. We were already moving into the shelter of the trees when he commenced singing softly the lines from a song just recently popular; '*yes I'm the son of hickory hollar's tramp*'

When the car ground to a halt beside the light, we could see that Bannaher was alone. He climbed out and looked slowly about him, shading his eyes as if to penetrate the gloom. *Over here you bastard, I'm over here.* He lit a cigar and his face was briefly illuminated. His eyes seemed to be staring straight at our hiding place. Unblinking, he must have held this pose for half a minute then the flame was extinguished. He knew we were there alright; it was almost as if he had smelt us. I suppressed a shiver. Without warning he dropped the hold-all he was carrying - literally dropped it - onto the light, then stepped briskly back into the car. In a moment he was heading back the way he had come, his rear lights bouncing crazily as he negotiated the bumpy road at speed.

We waited until the lights had vanished before retrieving the hold-all, kicking the light into the undergrowth before retreating into the trees. We jogged steadily for five minutes, not speaking, until we came to a clearing. Here, stood a disused hut, once used by forestry workers. Inside was my bike, our means of escape.

We didn't expect any trouble at this juncture, but you never knew. Whyte peered inside the hold-all then gave the thumbs-up sign. He quickly transferred the bundles of notes to a knapsack, stuffing the hold-all into a half-full water-butt at the rear of the hut.

By then I had wheeled the bike outside and fired her up. Soon we were moving through the forest. Almost silently it seemed, the sound deadened by the pine needles beneath us, and the branches that nearly enveloped us. We followed a path that we knew would take us over the hill and on to the main road, near the village of Rear Cross.

It was diagonally opposite to where we had picked up the money, and many miles from the route Bannaher had taken on his return, should he decide to try and ambush us. Quite frankly, we didn't know what he might do, but being Bannaher we knew that he wouldn't meekly pay up and leave it at that. It would have to be a time for very low profiles - and shut mouths. No problem there as far as I was concerned; I was baling out of this dump as soon as possible. I would enjoy spending Bannahers' money in London. Maybe even some of it at his old club.

To celebrate our success, we sank several pints in Durty Nellie's, listening in amusement as a fat American berated one of the barmen; 'Goddamit, haven't you heard of a Harvey Wallbanger? Tell me, do you know what a Screwdriver is?'

'I know what an American screwdriver is', he said as he served us. 'And I know what I'd like to do with it''

'I must be missing something'. I downed half my pint. 'What the fuck's an American screwdriver?'

'You don't know?' Whyte shook his head. 'What a sheltered life you've led. It's a tradesman's name for a hammer'.

'That explains it then. The one thing I've never been accused of is a tradesman'.

They were waiting for us when we got back. It was dark now, but a quarter moon hung sickle-like in the sky, creating a faint reflective glow around bright-coloured objects.

The first indication I had of the rope strung between the piers was when I looked at the gold balls sitting atop. If they had been the same colour as the piers I wouldn't have noticed a thing. As it was I was almost on them before I realised the rope was there. I had little time to do anything but instinctively duck. Whtye wasn't so lucky; I felt him being jerked from behind me, then I heard him hit the ground with a thud.

After that it became chaotic; somebody switched headlights on and I thought I saw Bannaher's visage in the reflected light behind them. I was like a rabbit trapped in the spotlight, dodging this way and that. I felt something strike my shoulder and I almost hit the deck. Somebody had swung a hurley at me, the heel of it connecting. Pain shot through me; I was sure my collar-bone was busted.

As I swung the bike around I saw Whyte rise to his feet. A leather-garbed figure hit him and he went down again. Fuck this for a game of soldiers, I thought, revving up. The bike shot forward and my outstretched leg connected with one of the assailants. He stayed upright and tried to grab me, but I kicked out again. Then I was through the piers, feeling solid tarmac under my wheel at last. I opened up the throttle and it was only as I hit the main Ennis road that I realised I hadn't seen or heard from Toni throughout the ordeal.

-

Christ, but Fishguard was a depressing hole. Especially at two am of a morning when you're waiting for the Paddington train to depart. The second coming ...or was it going? Jesus, what an ignominious departure, my tail between my legs. I owned nothing now except the clothes I stood up in and a few hundred quid in my pocket. The bike had been sold in Waterford for a lot less than it was worth - to a guy who quickly sized me up and decided that I needed the money more than he needed the Triumph. Ah well, that's life. Shat on from a great height once again.

It was now several days since I had run the gantlet at Lilac Creek - as I had christened Whyte's smallholding. Of the man himself there had been no word until I came across a few paragraphs in last night's Evening Herald. *'A Limerick man, Tom Whyte, was found knee-capped outside Limerick City last night. Police are making no comment at the moment, but it is thought to be punishment carried out by a paramilitary group. Whyte has been active in both trade union and political groups here and in England. His English-born wife Antonia said it was 'the work of savages'. She herself had been held hostage for several hours while the men lay in wait for her husband. A full report will be published later'.*

Of the money there had been no mention. It had been strapped to Whyte's back, so you could say that when he came off the bike it practically landed in Bannaher's lap. With hindsight, I suppose we had little chance of getting away with it. If we had known about Whyte and the rumours of stolen explosives in London, then so would Bannaher. All he had to do was put a watch on Whyte's place and wait for us to fall into the trap. Like a spider waiting for a fly.

I'd burnt my bridges for good now. There was no going back to Limerick or Croagh in the foreseeable future, not with the prospect of a knee-capping the only thing to look forward to.

# Chapter twenty

For two days now I've walked these mean streets; up Kilburn High Road, down Willesden Lane, round by the Jubilee Clock, and back through the fields to Cricklewood Broadway. Fields did I say? I've seen more grass on my ould fella's hobnailed boots when he was after walking the Croagh Road than I ever have since I lurched off the boat-train and got my first red-eyed glimpse of this concrete wilderness.

A drink, my kingdom for a drink. Passing The Case Is Altered now, the sweet aroma of strong porter rolling out its open doors. Oh Christ, there's a craving in me throat that won't be satisfied till I drench it with something stronger than water. Passing The Rising Sun, I thought I might cadge a free drink from some familiar face, till the barman caught sight of me and told me to keep moving. Maybe the White Horse will prove luckier. Did you ever hear empty pockets jangle? Ah Jasus, Chris, where are you? A few pounds is all I need to see me outa this bind.

There it is now. BARGAINS GALORE; SECOND-HAND FURNITURE BOUGHT AND SOLD. HOUSES CLEARED. The legend is plastered on a black-and-amber banner in letters a foot high over the shop-front. Chris's emporium. A tawdry collection of beds and cookers, tallboys and dressers, and stale mattresses stacked high against the rear wall. Nick-knacks clutter the shelves and window space; frosty china ornaments, stacks of mouldy books, clusters of LP's and tapes, several frying pans, and a teddy bear face down.

I rattle the door. Still locked. Christ, I've a pain in my shoulders from lying all night on a hard floor, and a rumbling in my stomach that sounds like distant thunder. A cup of tea...a nice warm cup of tea would be...

'Him don't open today, man'.

I turn to see a shiny black face bobbing up and down on shoulders a good six inches higher than mine. Dreadlocked ringlets, neatly braided, dance before my eyes.

'Me wanna sell him this radio, but the bloodclot don't come from his bed yet'.

I see the radio, wrapped in a brown paper bag, tucked under his arm. The paper is peeled back and a newish Phillips transistor is revealed..

'You wanna buy it, man? Five pounds'. White teeth gleam at me. 'New-brand, man'.

I laugh. 'I haven't got five pee, let alone a bloody fiver. I was hopin' yer man....' I indicate the doorway...'might lend me a few quid'.

'Him your frien'?'

'Not exactly'.

The dreadlocks dance again. 'Him a bloodclot thief, man. He thief alla' people who go to him. Last time him give me three pound for a radio and sell it for twelve...'

I come over faint and have to lean against the window. There's a reeling in my head.

'Man, you look terrible'. My companion is hunched over me now, peering into my face.

'Must be all that rich food I ate last night. You got the price of a cuppa?'

He feels in his pocket and presses a couple of coins in my palm. 'You're okay Paddy'. He nods at the shop. 'English?'

I shake my head. 'He's Irish just like me.'

He spits. 'Rassclot! What him thief alla' people for?' He wraps up the radio. 'Me come back later'.

'Hey!' I shout to his retreating back. 'If he's a thief, why do you deal with him?'

His teeth gleam again as he turns briefly. 'Me a thief too'.

*We're all thieves, man - it's just a question of degree.* This is the thought that pre-occupies me in the cafe a few doors along. I shovel four spoons of sugar into the cracked mug and drink half the tea straight down. After a few moments I feel more or less alive again. I learn from the woman behind the counter that Chris hasn't been seen around the shop for weeks. "I thinks he's sold it', she tells me, in between picking her nose. 'I hear he's bought a club. Rosalee's, I believe it's called. Just off the Broadway'.

'Rosie's', I say. Bannaher's old place. I'd barely recognised it when I'd first seen it.

'That's it, Rosie's. You know it, then?'

'Oh yes, I know it'. Not that fucking Chris had bought it though.

I wonder briefly how he can afford it, when I'm counting the pennies to see if I can afford a slice of toast to go with the tea. Fuck it, I order it anyway. I wolf it down in two bites then notice the Daily Mirror on the seat beside me. POWER WORKERS STRIKE LOOMS is the headline. I ignore all that crap and turn to the racing pages. Bad Man is running at Newmarket. Now there is a lay-down if I had the money. And Jim Jam Johnny at Haydock.

Hunched over my tea, I stare into the High Road. It's been two months since my return. Two months of lying low, drinking and gambling. And trying to suss out if Bannaher had put the word out on me. Nothing, sweet fuck-all, nobody has heard a thing. Fuck it, I can't go on like this; spending my days in William Hills, my nights in dives like Marnies, a barely-legit drinking club behind Stonebridge Park station.

I had already bumped into Bernie at Marnies, hardly recognising her.

'Hey Bernie', I say, when recognition has dawned, 'Is Chris still giving you the run-around?'

'Who gives a shit about that bastard? It's all change around here'.

I'd already noticed. The whole area was being pulled down. Whole streets were being flattened from Stonebridge Park to Willesden. The slums were being shoveled into tipper trucks and fly-tipped all over the Capital. Even the Ace Cafe was boarded up.

It is all change with Bernie too; eyes as black as a Panda, hair long and straight, and a black dress that has been doled out by the square inch.

'Mine's a Bacardi', she adds.

Pushing my way in the semidarkness through the small group of bodies gyrating on what is laughingly called the dance floor, I see one or two familiar faces. No Larry or Chris though. Not surprising really. The Last Chance Saloon we called it in the days when we weren't too fussy where we wet our whistles. You had to be either desperate or pissed to come here. Still, it was nice to find one citadel of stability in this turbulent world!

I return with the drinks to find Bernie half-sprawled against a table; one long, silky thigh completely shorn of covering. Already half-stoned by the look of her.

'Let's dance'. She grabs me, then pauses and gulps down most of the Bacardi before dragging me into the maelstrom. She gulps down something else too.

As a dance team we aren't very original. Her hands encircle my neck, while her mouth nuzzles it. My hands rest on her hips, meshing our groins together. Dance steps are minimal; a sort of slow erotic lurch, that is clearly headed in only one direction.

'What was it like being without a woman for two years?' I can feel her teeth nibbling on my earlobe as she whispers the question.

'Twice as bad as being without one for one year'. I don't bother correcting her misapprehension about the length of my sentence. I can feel her nudging my cock. Sizing it up?

This is my first contact with Bernie for almost three years. My first close contact in all the time I had known her. I didn't count the night - or part of a night - we'd shared my bed. She had completely freaked out, fainted, or pretended to, when I eventually got her knickers off. I think she only hopped under the blankets with me hoping that Chris would turn up before I shoved my dick up her. Well, he hadn't. And I hadn't either. Necrophilia didn't appeal to me. I rolled over and had a quiet wank...and when I woke up next morning she had gone.

'Seen Chris lately?', I ask her now.

'That bastard! Not for ages. We don't move in the same circles anymore'. She nudges me again. 'I can get some...you know...stuff. It keeps you going all night'.

Jesus! Is this the same Bernie? I thought she'd be up to her elbows in babies and shitty nappies by now. Instead, all that interests her is uppers and downers.

We do keep going all night. What I can remember of it. A phrase keeps coming into my mind; re-headed women buck like goats. Now where had I read that? I look at Bernie, snoring peacefully beside me: I guess the same is true of black-haired ones.

There's a rattling on the door. 'Bernie, it's nearly nine. Are you getting up for Mass?'

Bloody hell! It's Sunday. I hope she doesn't expect me to go.

Bernie is awake now, disheveled, crawling about the bed, looking for something. She stubs her toe and swears, sees me and gives a little squeal. The sudden movement is too much, her hand go to her head and she moans, 'me head, me feckin' head'.

I can't resist cupping her breasts. She squeals again.

'Have you got someone in there? I'll come back in a few minutes'.

Bernie disappears into the bathroom to throw up. She is back moments later looking like something out of Madam Tussaud's. I get up and make us some coffee, which she sips as she struggles into her Sunday clothes.

'Oh God, I'm mortified. That was Liz. All the girls at work will know tomorrow'. Work was Smiths, near Staples Corner, where she assembled radios.

She returns from Mass all sanctified, barley letting me kiss her. When I try to slip my hands between her thighs, she slaps it away. 'What do you think you're doing? I'm only after coming back from Mass'.

'Sorry. I forgot the eleventh commandment. Saturday night's okay, but thou shalt not fuck on Sunday'.

'I had too much to drink last night'.

*Isn't it always the same with women after they've opened their legs? You got me drunk...I wasn't myself...a being from outer space took over my body...*

-

London on the Sabbath is a strange place. Silent, almost ghostlike, streets deserted except for the occasional dog-walker or car-polisher. Weird nation the Sassenachs; they think more of their dogs and their cars than they do their children. I tried to visualise the same scene taking place in Croagh and couldn't. The dog would be given a kick up the arse and sent yelping across the fields, and if it rained...well, the car got washed.

Passing Rosies, I decide to go in. Bernie is strangely reluctant. I almost have to drag her past the bouncer. Past the glitter and gloss of freshly-painted interiors; constructed from job lots of chipboard and skirting board diverted from building sites out Harrow and Hendon way; decorated using gallons of paint conveniently slipped off the back of some Wembley-bound lorry or Transit.

'What's the matter with you? I want to see what the old place looks like now that Bannaher has gone'.

'Let's go to Marnie's', she pleads. 'There's nothing for you here'.

*Oh, but there is, Bernie. There is. Coming here is a rejuvenating experience. I feel alive when I look around me and see how things might have been. Weary and bent from too many days spent down too many damp holes, coming back to places like this and pissing it all against the wall, that's my lot if I let the lump grind me down. The triumph of hope over experience, Bernie, that's what brings me back.*

I look around and see one or two vaguely familiar faces. Slicked-back heads, curly and shining with hair-oil, line the bar, thin ties trawling the counter as animated faces converse in claustrophobic huddles, breaking off only long enough to raise their eyes heavenwards before taking another lungful of Guinness on board. Behind them, women hover, in their long sleeves and short skirts, knees held primly together, the vacuous looks on their faces broken by the occasional shrill laugh or exclamation. Tomorrow, they will be back in more familiar surroundings; the women to the sweatshops of Neasden or Cricklewood, soldering knobs on radios or some other riveting task; the men spitting on their hands and polishing their shovels as they contemplate their version of trench warfare.

To say Rosie's has had a facelift would be an understatement. Its guts have been ripped out; the hole-in-the-wall appearance favoured by Bannaher jack-hammered out of existence, the bare floorboards and non-matching furniture replaced by plush carpets and chrome seating. The serving area has been reduced too; it is now an island in the middle of the floor. An oasis where the punters can expensively slake their thirsts.

I look to see if the framed mementoes of Bannaher's tenure still adorn the back wall; the crossed hurleys, the blown-up photos of him being embraced by a posse of bishops and politicians. They don't. But then, the back wall is no longer in its original position. It has been moved back fifty feet, to the boundaries of what had once been the back garden. The intervening area has been concreted over and floored in a mosaic of gold and brown wood. It is so highly polished you can almost see your reflection in it. The new ceiling glitters with an array of strobe lights, eager to envelop would-be dancers in a rainbow of colours.

Dougie had lived under that floor for a month or more. Poor Dougie. I wonder what he is doing now. If he is doing anything at all. I have heard rumours that he was run over by a bus on the Kilburn High Road, staggering out from an off-licence. So maybe he is six feet under for real now.

Bernie is right. This isn't my scene anymore.

'Come on', I say, 'we'll try Marnie's'.

As we take our departure, a strange ritual is being enacted in the entrance lobby. The bouncer is propelling a much smaller man in circles, then laughing as he staggers away.

'I've got a tie', the smaller one gasps, 'it's in my pocket'.

'It's not your tie, sir. You've had too much drink taken'.

"Let me see the owner. I'm a friend of the owner...'

It is only when they waltz under the light that I recognise the smaller man as Larry. Then he is gone, as the bouncer tires of the game and propels him headlong out the door. I see a number sixteen bus lumber by and fear the worst.

We follow him out and I see that a lamp post has halted his progress. I help him to his feet. He drags a cigarette from somewhere, manages to set fire to it then inhales it like it was pure oxygen, all the time clinging to the post to stay upright.

People age, time sees to that, but in Larry's case something had speeded up the process. He was thirty five, going on fifty. The craggy jaw, the features once likened to Jack Nicklaus, had crumpled inexplicably, the bone structure buried in the folds of flesh under his chin. His eyes were wide and wild looking, the wildness accentuated by the sagging pockets underneath them. A lot of his hair had fallen out, most of his front teeth were missing, and those that weren't were a yellowy-brown.

I see him squint a few times as he studies me then he stops twitching. The effort of standing is too much and he begins to slide down the post. There is a dwarf wall nearby and I help him to it.

'It's not all drink you know'. He grins lopsidedly. 'Oh, I know I'm a physical wreck, but....', he slaps at his left leg,… 'this doesn't help'.

I'd noticed the limp as he had shuffled across the pavement.

He grins again. 'They tell me I was lucky. I have more metal inside my leg than the Tin Man, and they tell me I was lucky. You should have seen the car...'

'What happened?'

'Was I pushed or did I jump, hah?' He seems confused to me. 'Bang!...a year ago, maybe more. After she bought me off and kicked me out...' His voice trails off, perhaps remembering that 'she' had a lot to do with our acrimonious parting. 'I married your woman', he says, finally.

'She was never m y woman, Larry'.

'She's not mine now either. The fucking bitch bought me off...then threw me out'.

I gradually piece it together. Tessa had offered him five thousand for his share in everything, including the house. By that time they weren't living together anymore, and she was paying all the bills anyway. When he tried to haggle she told him to take it or leave it. He took it. A couple of days later he found his belongings in the garage and all the locks changed.. He bought himself a souped-up Ford for a couple of grand, and created quite a stir around the pubs and clubs of NW London for a few months. Until the night he'd wrapped the Ford around a column that was part of the new flyover at Staples Corner.

'All that's left now is a few hundred...and this pile of nuts and bolts in me leg'.

'What about compensation?'

'Insurance on the car? You must be joking'. He lights another cigarette and coughs up a storm. 'It's not the cough that carries you off, it's the coffin they carry you off in, wha?' Another grin. 'Seen anything of Bannaher lately?'

'No'.

'I heartell he's asking after you. The Crown, The Nags Head, all the ould haunts, they've all had inquiries about your whereabouts'.

'I'm sure they have. Well, Bannaher can go fuck himself'.

'I wouldn't worry too much about him. There's not many round this town would piss on him if he was on fire'. He tries another grin. 'We had some good times round this kip, didn't we Terry'.

'Yeah'. Didn't we fuck.

Larry looks slightly embarrassed. 'Do you know what I was doing in there?' He indicates Rosie's. 'I was hoping to see Chris. I heard tell there might be a job going'.

I look at Bernie and she shrugs.

'Doing what?'

'Collecting glasses and stuff...' He looks at me. 'Well, I'm not exactly Charles Atlas these days...'

Later, having seen him safely back to the basement flat he occupies in Thomas Road, I say to Bernie. 'Collecting glasses for Chris for fuck sake...!'

Later still, having sampled the fare in a number of places, including Marnie's and The Black Lion, we feast on a brunch at the Wimpey Bar on the High Road, then put down a few minutes at the tea dance in the Banba. This doesn't appeal to either of us so we get a taxi back to Bernie;s place and get our heads down for a few hours.

I'm only killing time, and I suspect Bernie knows, because she becomes all mawkish and asks me to stay the night. I say why not, and we fall asleep locked together in a post-coital embrace.

It is our intention to go out later on, but we oversleep. Instead, we wind up getting maudlin in front of the TV, over a litre of wine bought from the nearby off-licence.

'He's a no-good bastard', Bernie slurs.

'No', I agree.

'What'ya mean, no?'

'I mean yes'.

'He's going places, he says'.

'All the wrong places'.

'Putting Rosie's on the map, he says'.

'Fuck Rosie's'.

'Would you...is she really the love of your life?'

'Who?'

'Tessa?'

'Once maybe, not now'.

'She and Larry didn't hit it off. She was sweet on you though'.

' Is that so?'

'They say she has a mansion in Ireland now. All la-di-dah'.

'All la-di-dah'.

'Where's the money come from?'

'Where's anyone's money come from? Other people, that's where'.

'I think I'm going to be sick'.

'So am I'.

-

That was over a week ago. I haven't seen Bernie since. I went round to her place and the landlady said she was in hospital. Some sort of overdose, she said. 'I can't keep her room for ever you know. Her rent was due last Saturday'.

I phoned the hospital and they said she was going to be okay. But I can't face seeing her. Not yet. I also phoned Rosie's and asked to speak to Chris.

'Mr Webster is in America at present', a plummy voice informed me. 'Can I take a message, sir?'

'Yes', I said, 'tell him go and fuck himself''.

-

I finish my tea and wave the woman in the cafe goodbye, cursing the drizzle as I make my way along Willesden Lane. Tomorrow morning I am taking my one good trousers and my one pair of sturdy boots and this aching body of mine along to the Crown to look for the start. I am still young and strong, still able to swing a pick and shovel with the best of those bastards. A few weeks is all I need to get back on my feet again. But first a drink. Jesus, I could kill for a drink. I know, I'll go and see Larry. He's sure to have a few bob in his pocket.

It'll be like old times again.

**end**

# About the Author

Tom O'Brien is a native of Kilmacthomas, Co Waterford, Ireland and is a full time writer and playwright.

Performed plays include **Money from America, Cricklewood Cowboys, On Raglan Road. Johnjo, Gorgeous Gaels, Behan's Women, Down Bottle Alley, Kathy Kirby - Icon** etc Copies of his plays can be emailed to interested parties.

Published books include **Confessions of an Altar Boy, Confessions of a Corner Boy, Cassidy's Cross, Down Bottle Alley, The Shiny Red Honda, The Missing Postman and Other Stories**

Tom has lived in Hastings UK since 2000.

Printed in Poland
by Amazon Fulfillment
Poland Sp. z o.o., Wrocław

62047855R00096